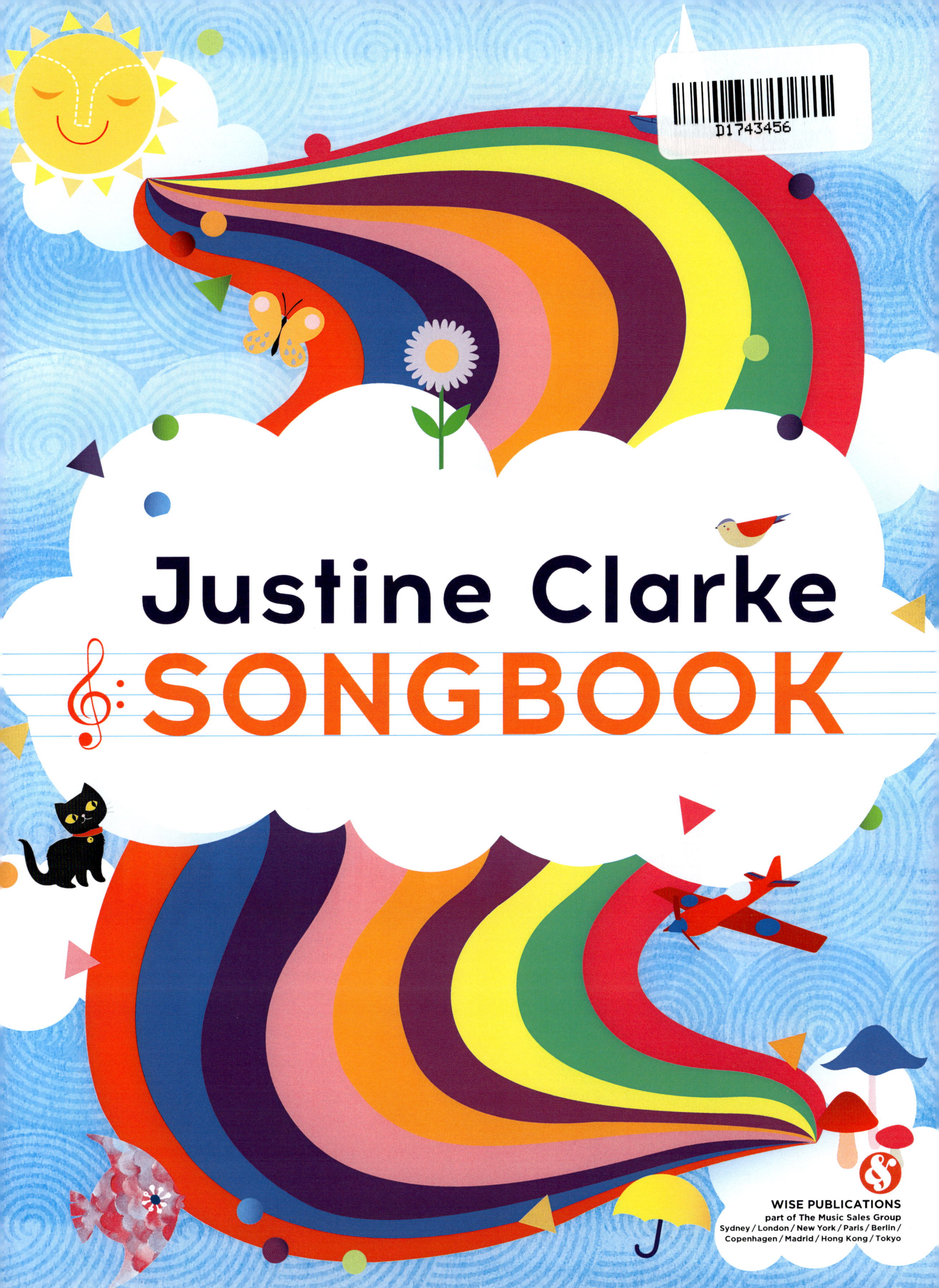

Justine Clarke
SONGBOOK

WISE PUBLICATIONS
part of The Music Sales Group
Sydney / London / New York / Paris / Berlin /
Copenhagen / Madrid / Hong Kong / Tokyo

Published by
Wise Publications
14-15 Berners Street, London W1T 3LJ, UK.

Exclusive Distributors:
Music Sales Pty Limited
4th floor, Lisgar House, 30-32 Carrington Street,
Sydney, NSW 2000, Australia.

Music Sales Limited
Distribution Centre, Newmarket Road,
Bury St Edmunds, Suffolk IP33 3YB, UK.

Music Sales Corporation
180 Madison Avenue, 24th Floor,
New York NY 10016, USA.

Order No. AM1012022
ISBN: 978-1-78558-343-8
This book © Copyright 2017 Wise Publications,
a division of Music Sales Limited.

Illustrations and design by Beci Orpin.
Additional design and pre-production by Tim Field.
Music arranged by Peter Dasent.
Music edited by Toby Knowles.
Music processed by Sarah Lofthouse, SEL Music Art Ltd.
Cover photo and page 58 photo courtesy of Lisa Tomasetti.
Page 5 photo courtesy of Gen Kay.
With special thanks to Justine Clarke and Sonia Le.

Printed in Australia.

Your Guarantee of Quality:

As publishers, we strive to produce every book
to the highest commercial standards.

This book has been carefully designed to minimise awkward page
turns and to make playing from it a real pleasure.

Particular care has been given to specifying acid-free, neutral-sized paper
made from pulps which have not been elemental chlorine bleached. This pulp is from
farmed sustainable forests and was produced with special regard for the environment.

Throughout, the printing and binding have been planned to ensure a sturdy,
attractive publication which should give years of enjoyment.

If your copy fails to meet our high standards,
please inform us and we will gladly replace it.
www.musicsales.com

www.justineclarke.com.au

Introduction

Hi there!

Here is a collection of selected songs from the nearly 50 songs composed and produced by Peter Dasent, in collaboration with Arthur Baysting, plus various other very talented lyricists (including myself!) from the albums *I Like To Sing*, *Songs To Make You Smile* and *Great Big World*.

When we first recorded *I Like To Sing*, we had no idea if anyone would play it. We just wanted to make an album of songs we liked to listen to.

Today, there are families with teenagers and families with toddlers who count 'Watermelon' or 'Dinosaur Roar' as the most familiar and much-loved song during their pre-school years. We are so happy to be releasing this songbook of the top 16 songs from all 3 albums.

Over the years, there have been countless requests for the sheet music for these songs. So, it's with great pride, excitement and relief that this book has finally arrived! We get so much feedback about how the songs are used in early childhood education, at home or at parties and it gives us great joy to know that you can now accompany yourselves or use this book to help others to learn the joy of playing music. The arrangements are designed to be played by anyone with basic ability on the piano, guitar or ukulele and, in a couple of cases, they have been altered to a more suitable key for kids to sing.

These days, children's music is more a visual medium than ever and throughout the book you will notice familiar motifs and colourful images from all the albums. We wanted this music book to be fun to look at too!

At the heart of this book is a genuine love of music and a desire to share songs that every age group can enjoy together. Our voices are our first instrument and the key to the beginning of a lifelong appreciation of music. We hope you enjoy singing and playing these songs as much as we do. Perhaps it will inspire you to write your own songs too!

Enjoy!

Justine, Peter and Arthur

Creatures of the Rain & Sun

Words by Arthur Baysting
Music by Peter Dasent

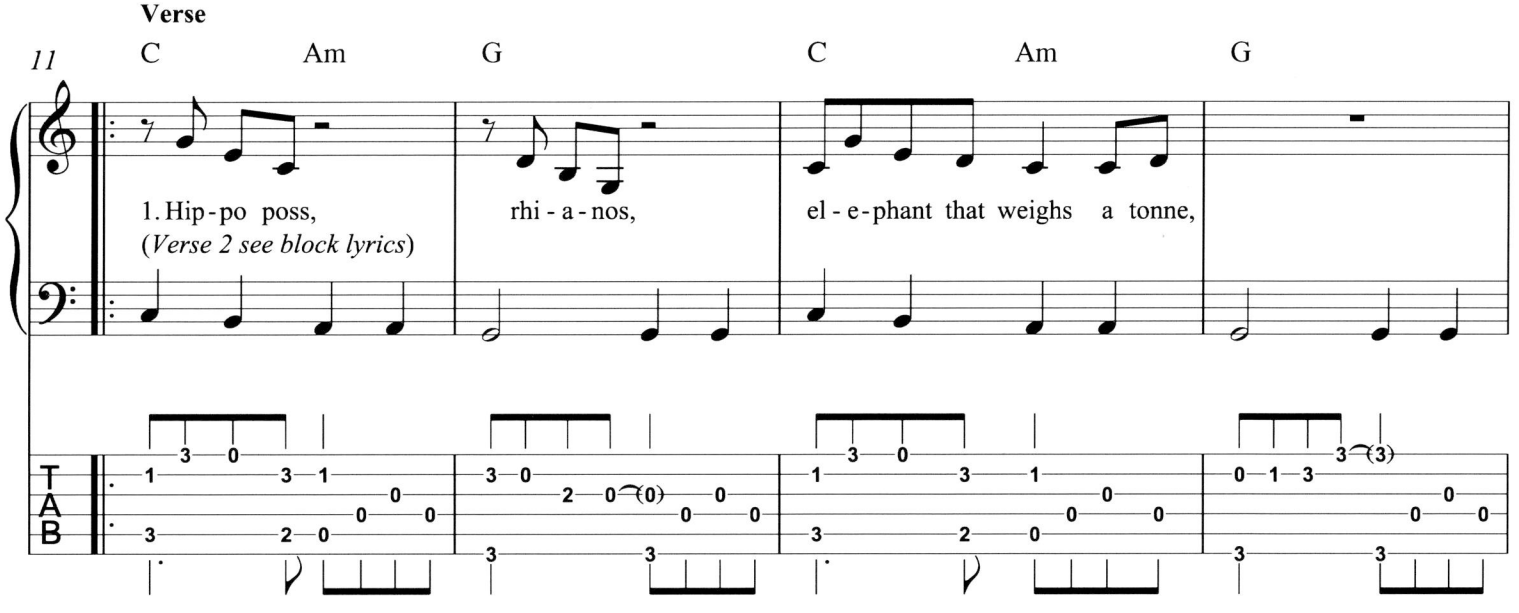

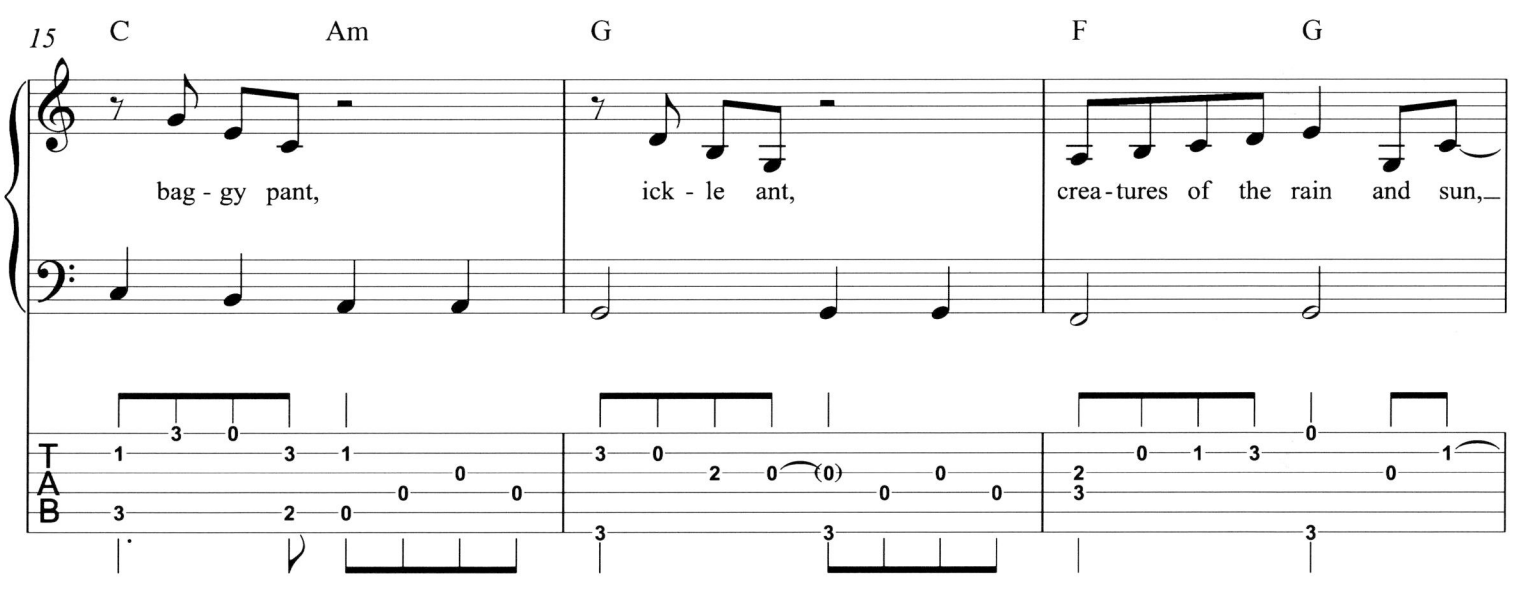

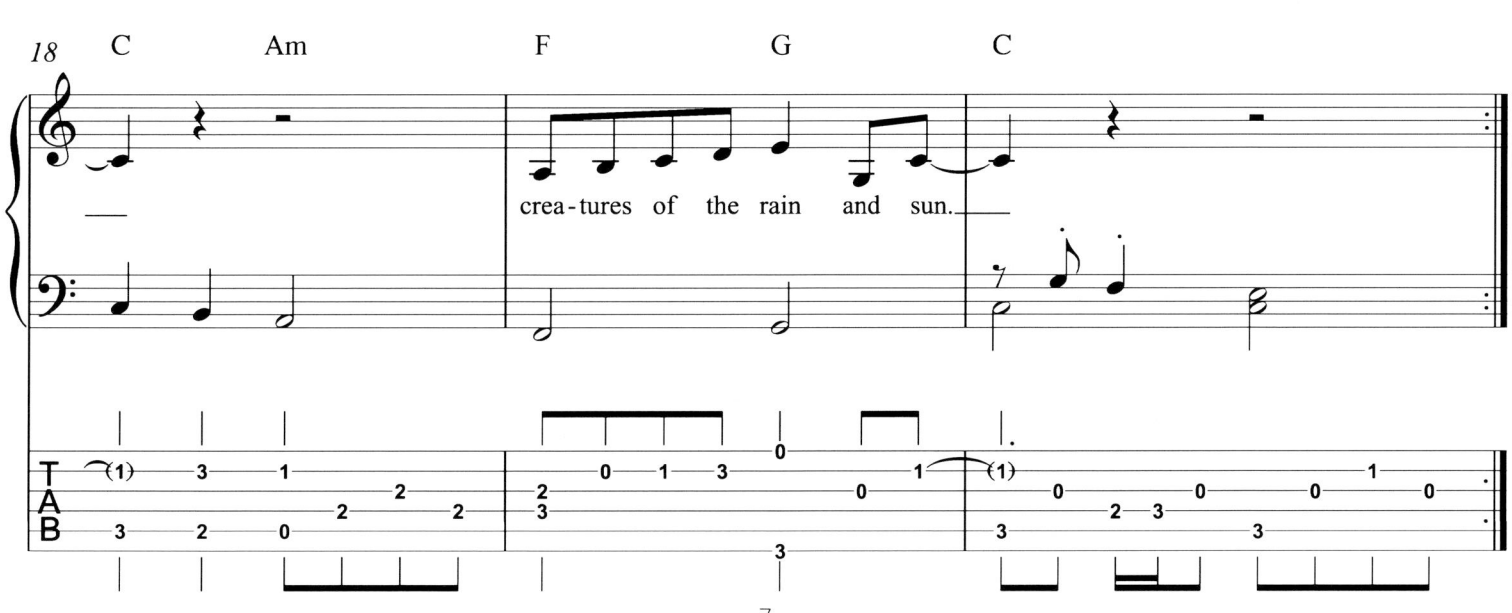

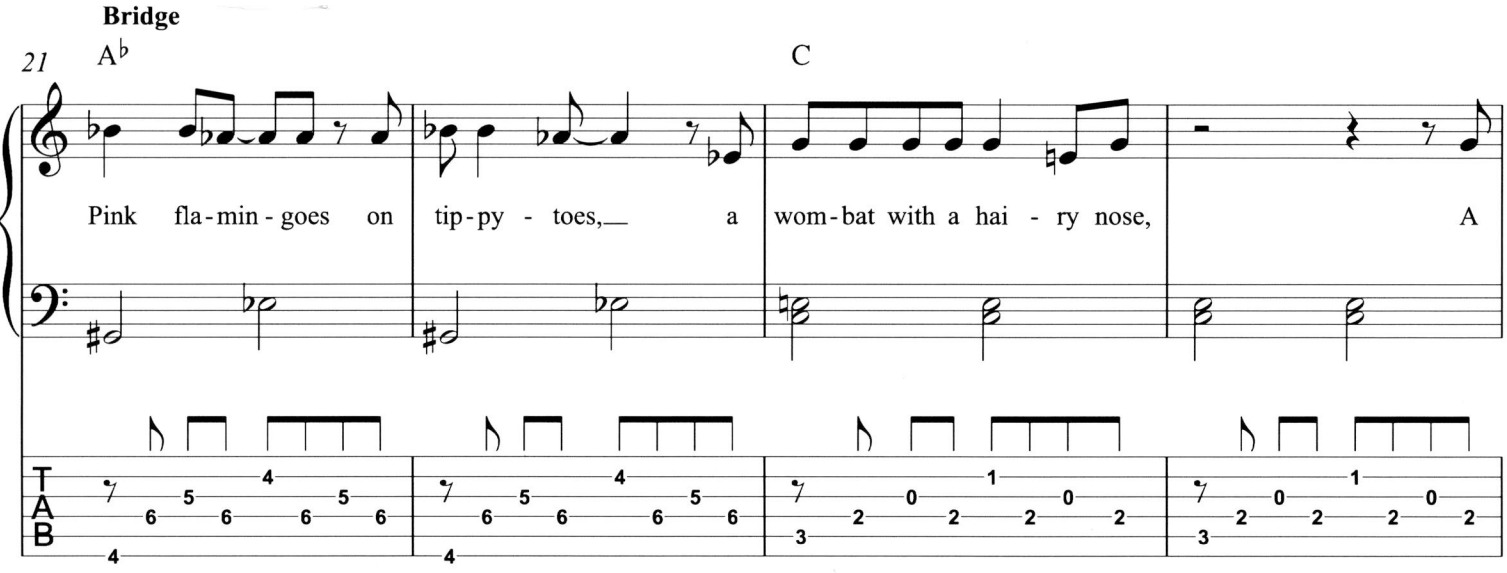

Bridge

Pink fla-min-goes on tip-py-toes,___ a wom-bat with a hai - ry nose, A

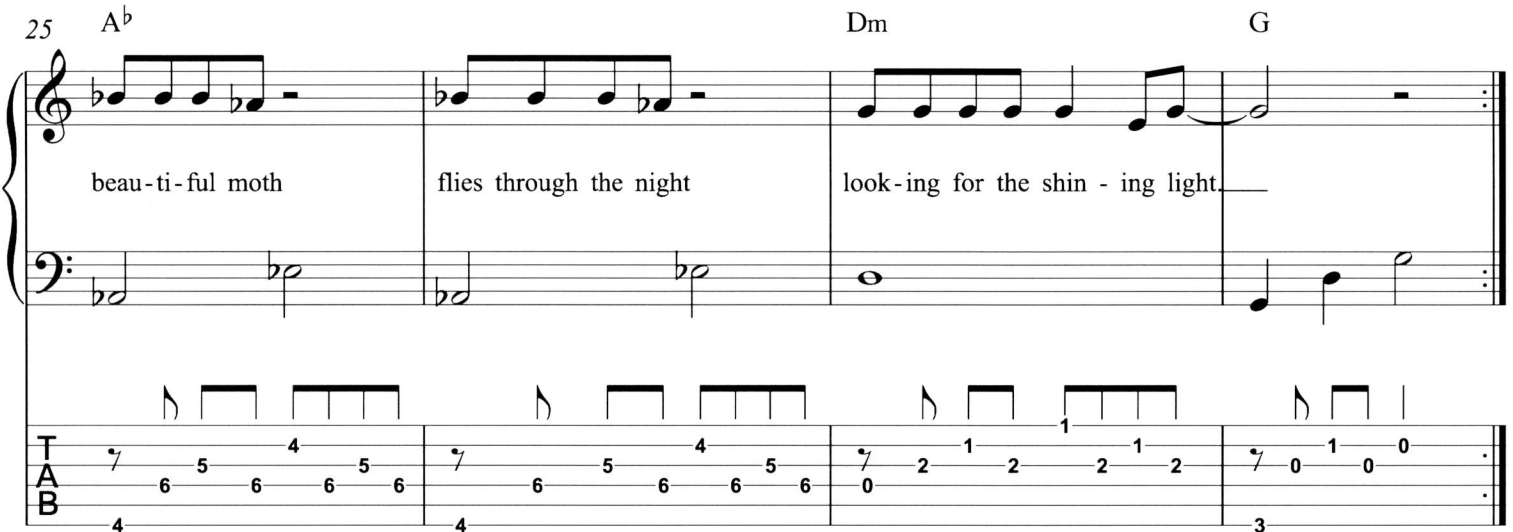

beau-ti-ful moth flies through the night look-ing for the shin - ing light.___

Verse 1:
Hippo-pos, rhi-a-nos, elephant that weighs a ton,
Baggy pant, ickle ant,
Creatures of the rain and sun,
Creatures of the rain and sun.

Verse 2:
Dragon fly, flying by, monkey with a purple bottom,
Kangaroo, moo-cow moo,
Creatures of the rain and sun,
Creatures of the rain and sun.

Bridge:
Pink flamingos on tippy toes,
A wombat with a hairy nose,
A beautiful moth flies through the night,
Looking for a shining light.

Verse 3:
Tiny bug, slimy slug, little puppy having fun,
Pussy cat, flying bat,
Creatures of the rain and sun,
Creatures of the rain and sun.

Verse 4:
Pretty bird of paradise,
Seagulls chewing chocolate buns,
You and me and everyone,
Creatures of the rain and sun,
Creatures of the rain and sun.

Dancing Face

Words by Arthur Baysting
Music by Peter Dasent

You can walk and talk, you can dance and sing,

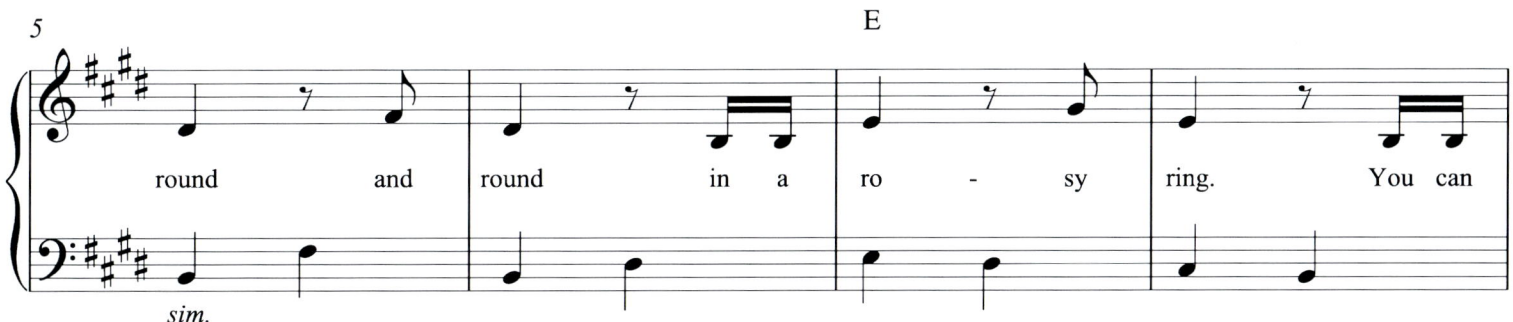

round and round in a ro - sy ring. You can

swim in the sea, you can fly through space but

can you make a danc-ing face.

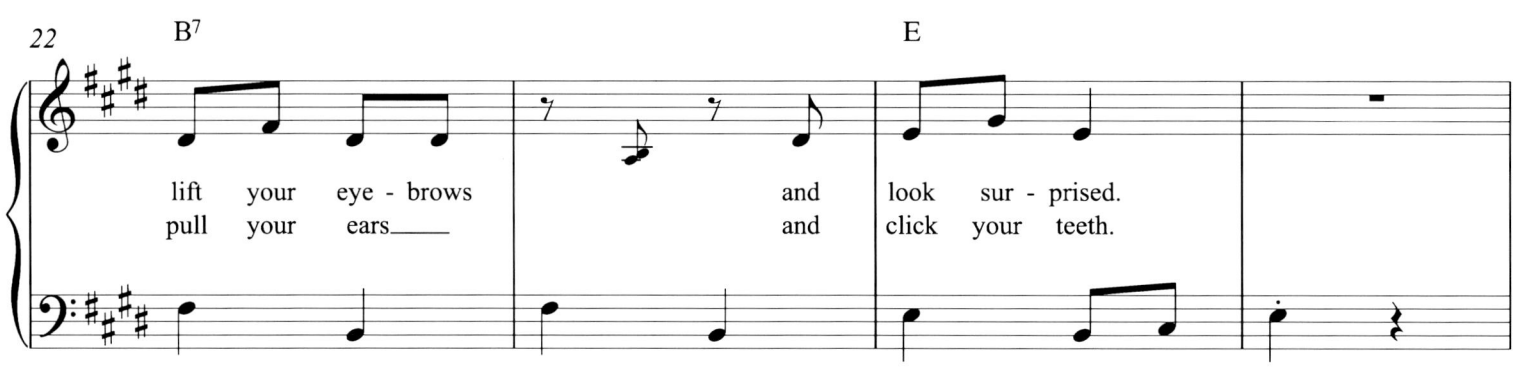

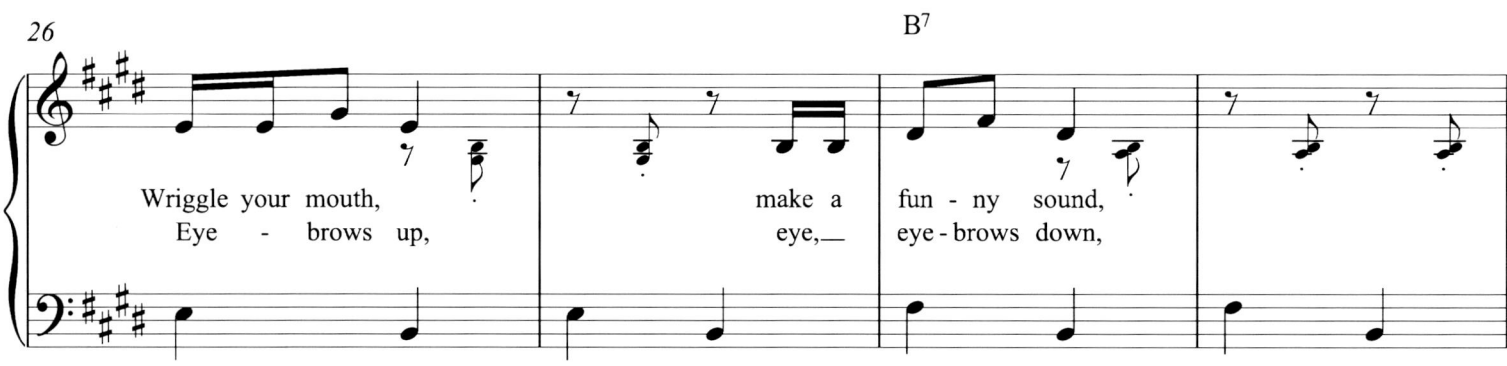

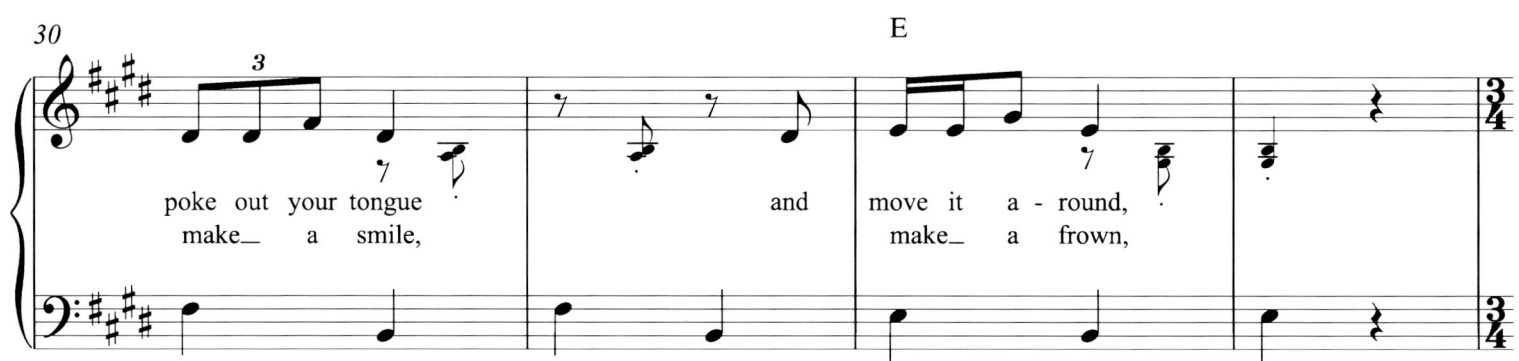

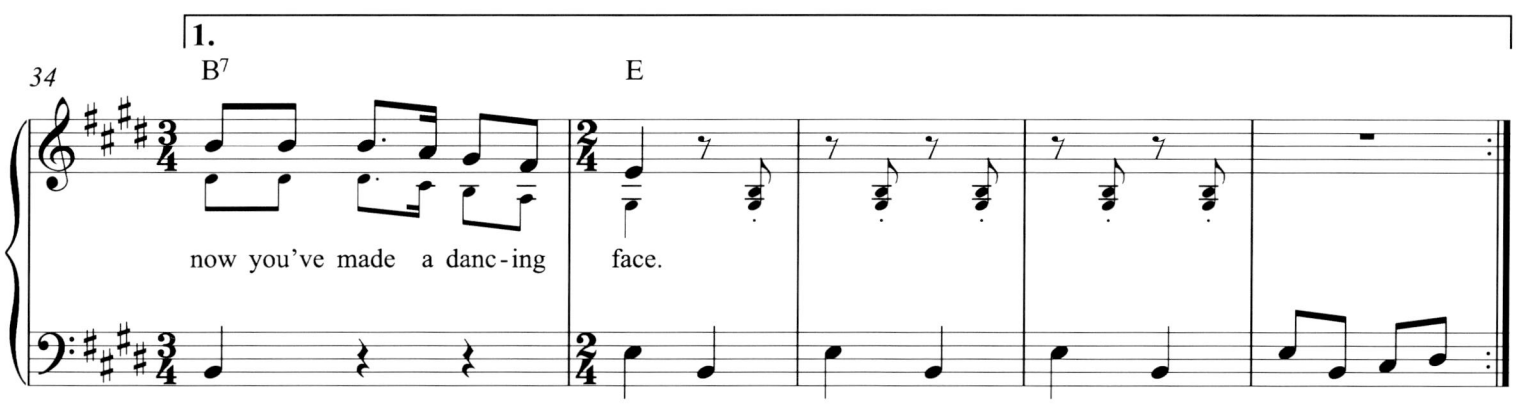

now you've made a danc-ing face.

put it to - ge - ther it's all it takes for

you to make a danc-ing face, danc-ing face,

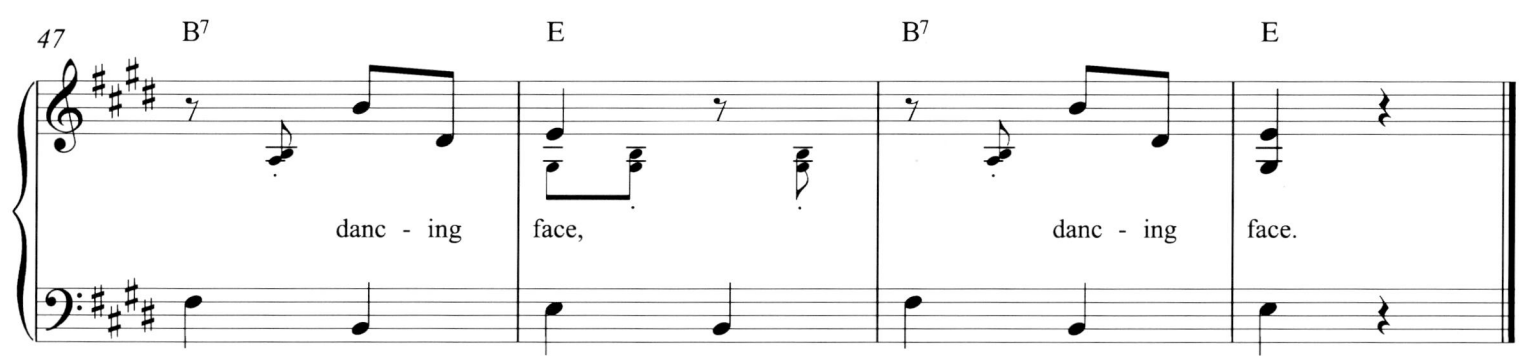

danc-ing face, danc-ing face.

Dancing Pants

Words by Arthur Baysting and Justine Clarke
Music by Peter Dasent

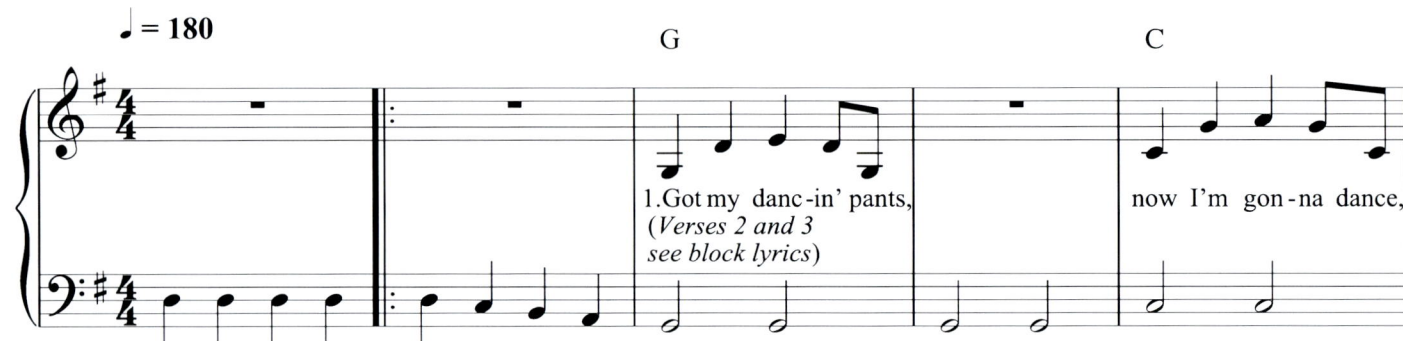

1.Got my danc-in' pants,
(*Verses 2 and 3*
see block lyrics)
now I'm gon-na dance,

won't you come a-long   danc-ing to this song.

Let's try this and see   mov-ing with our feet,   do it af-ter me

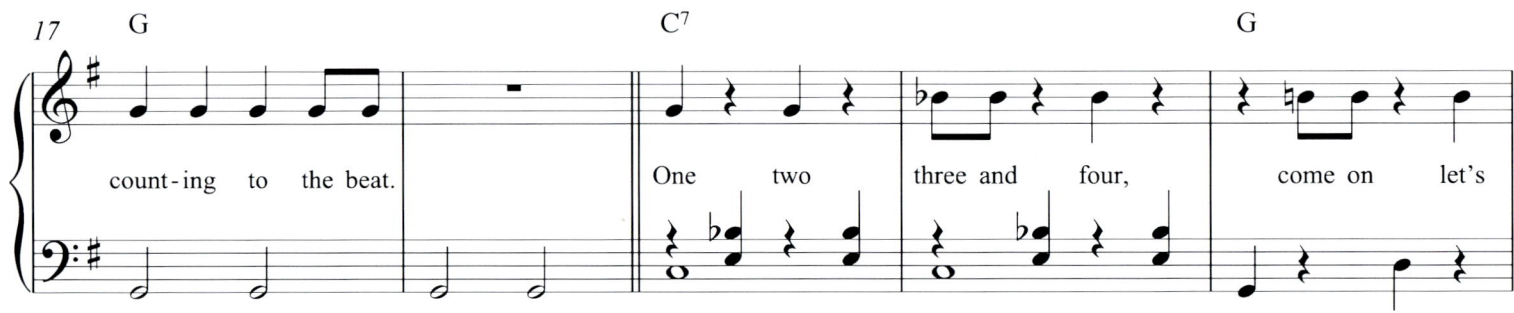

count-ing to the beat.   One two three and four,   come on let's

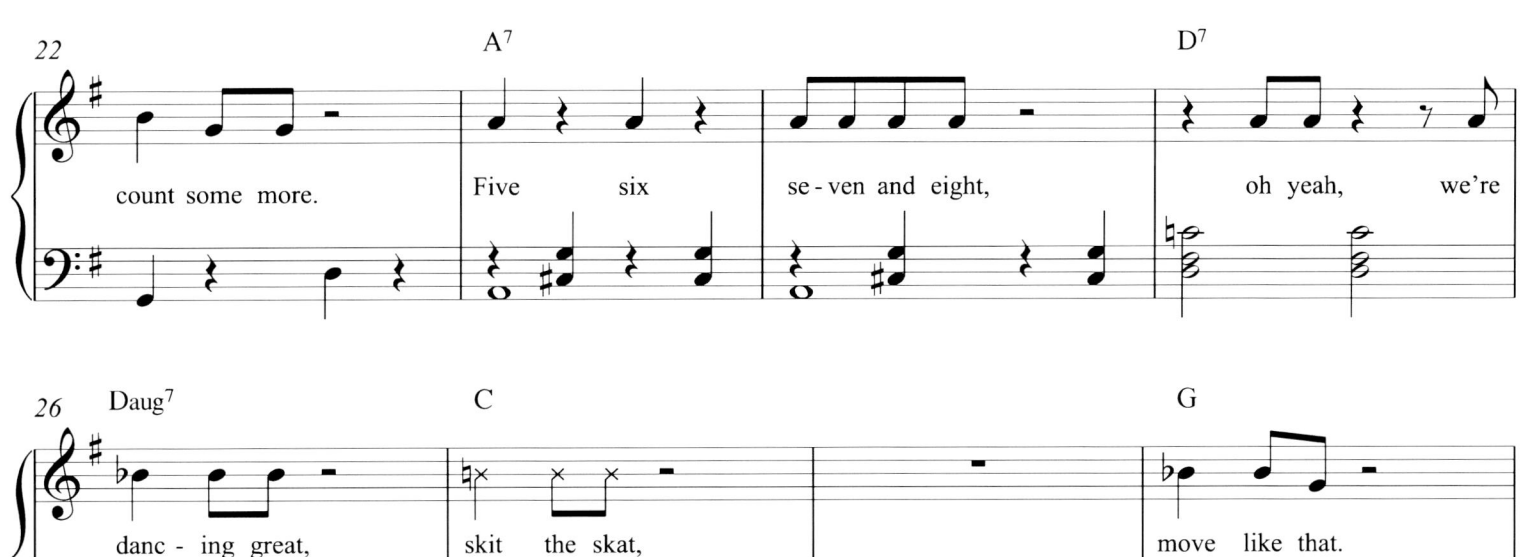

Verse 2:
Hands float through the air, climbing up a tree,
Slowly turn around, clap your hands with me,
Feet stuck on the floor, then we move our knees,
Moving back and forth, dancin' to the beat.

1 2 3 and 4, come on let's count some more,
5 6 7 8 and 9, let's try something new this time,
Bump the bump, and tip your hat,
Zabbity bop and shoo shaboom,
Let's all move and groove across the room.

Uh-huh-huh!

Verse 3:
If you wanna dance, grab your dancin' pants,
Do your belt up tight, now you're dancin' right.
Kick your feet up high, try and touch the sky,
Shake shake shake your hair, shout out loud – yeah yeah yeah!

1 2 3 and 4, come on let's count some more,
5 6 7 8 9 10, put it all together again.
Skit the skat, move like that,
Bump the bump, tip the hat,
Zabbedy bop, shoo sh'boom.
Let's all move and groove across the room.

Dancin' Pants.

Dinosaur Roar

Words by Arthur Baysting and Justine Clarke
Music by Peter Dasent

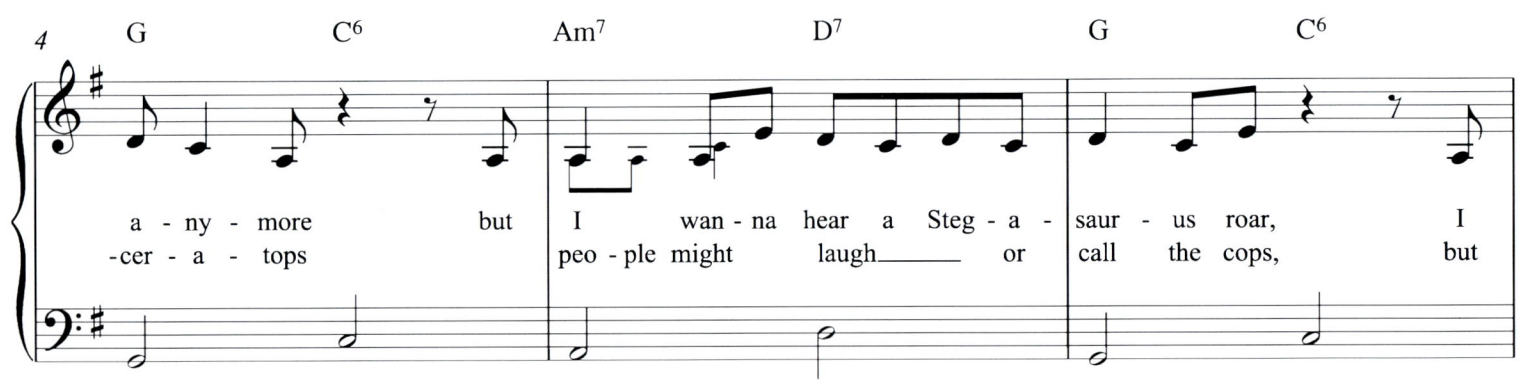

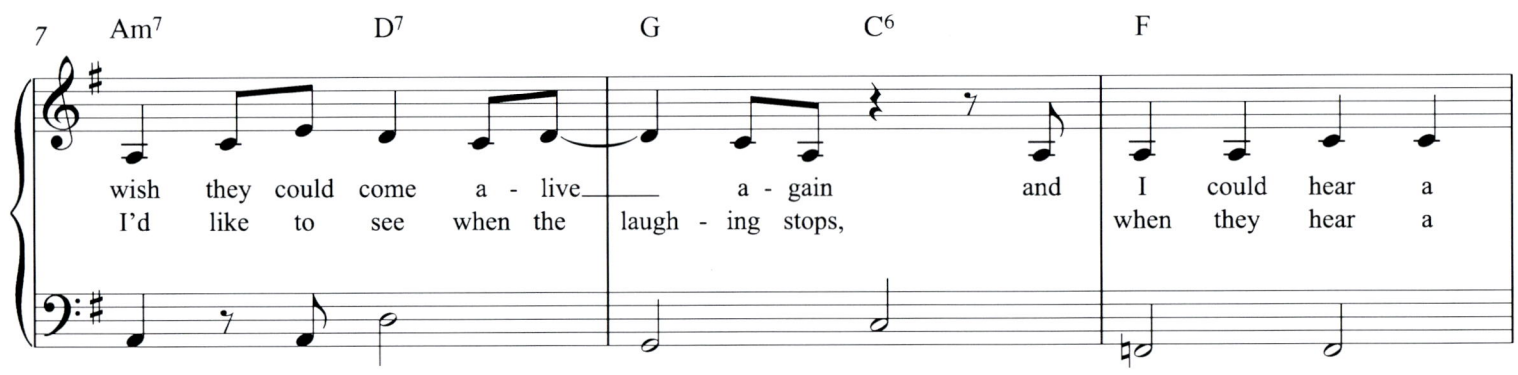

real   di - no-saur   roar!
real   Tri - cer - a   tops   roar!

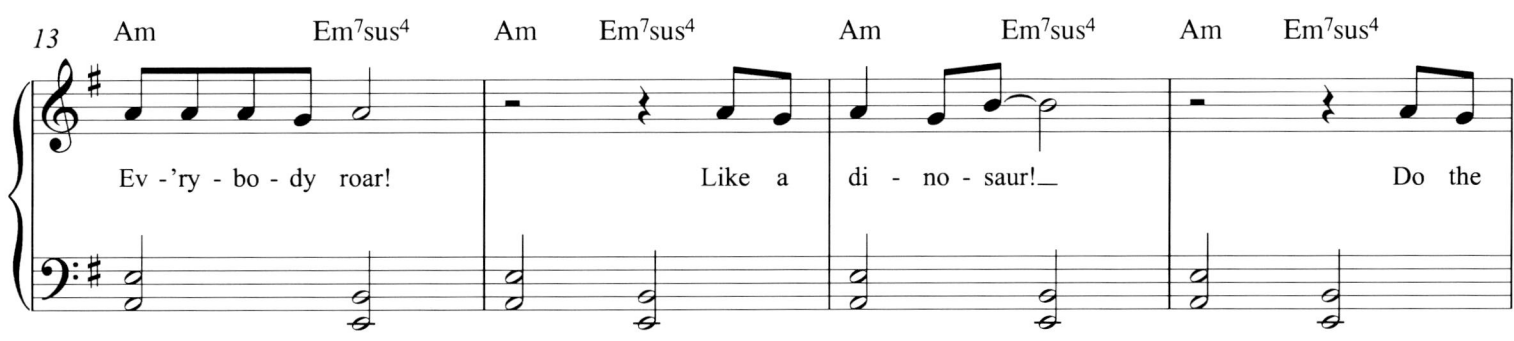

Ev -'ry-bo-dy roar!   Like a   di - no-saur!_   Do the

1.

di - no - saur   roar!   2. If they

2.

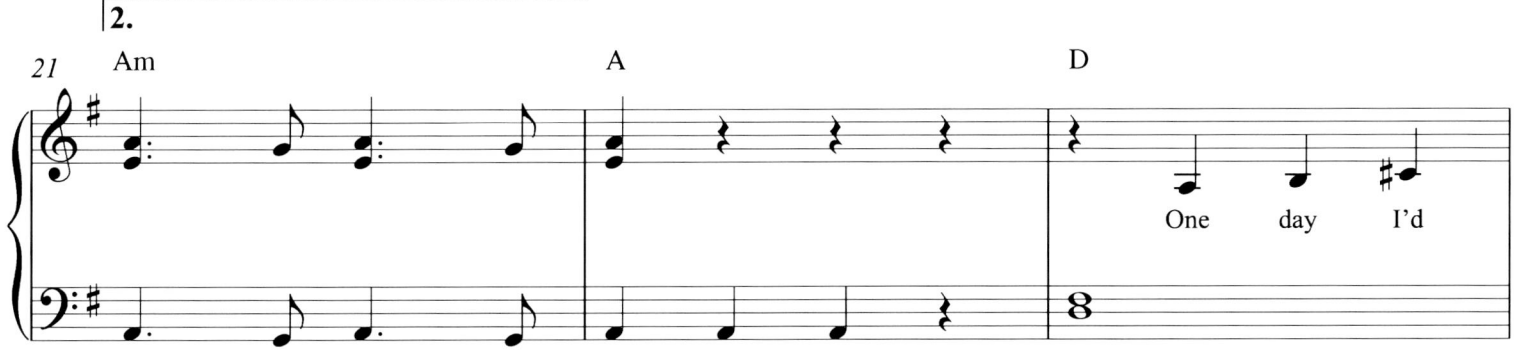

One   day   I'd

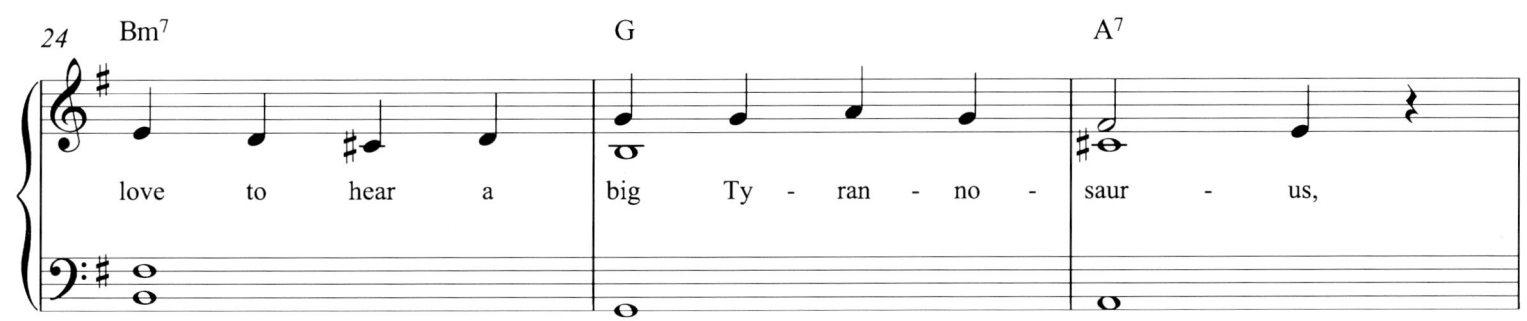

love   to   hear   a   big   Ty - ran - no -   saur -   us,

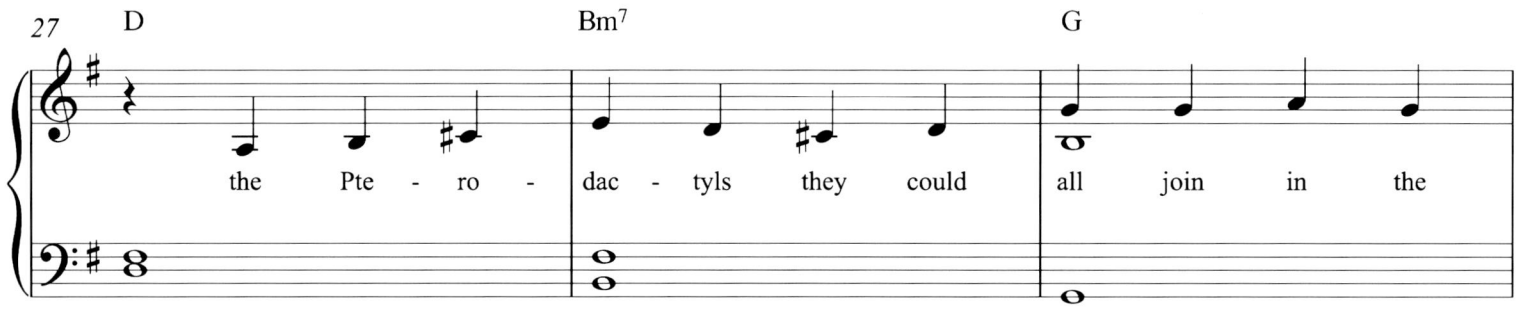

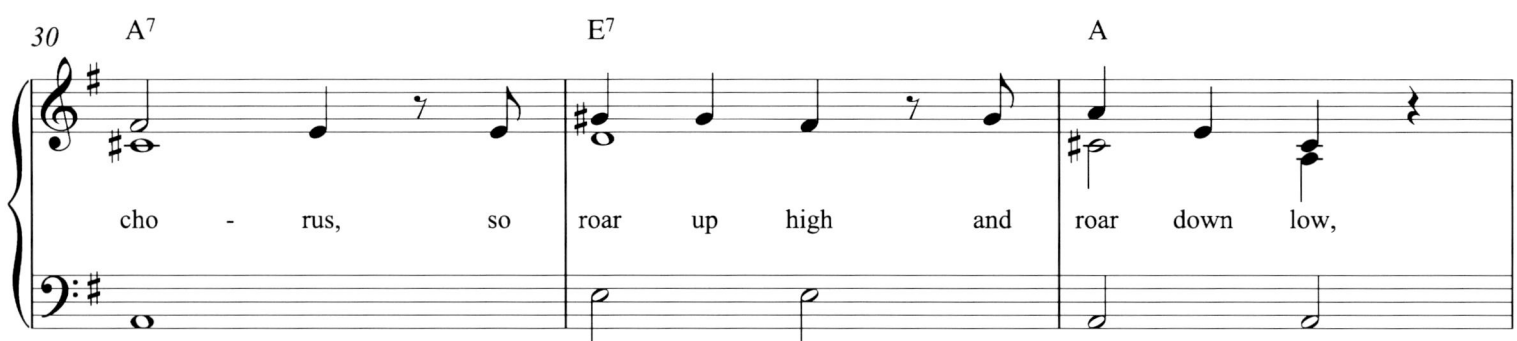

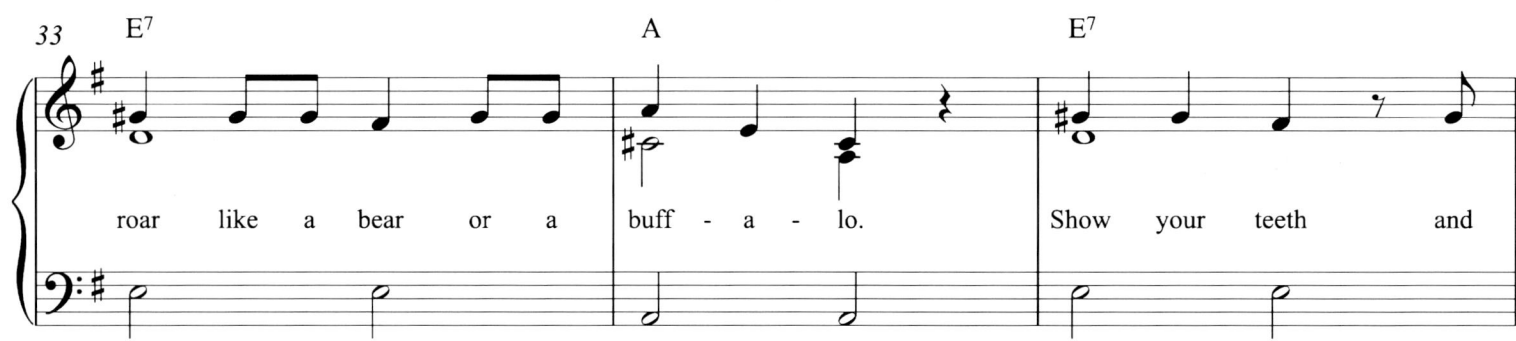

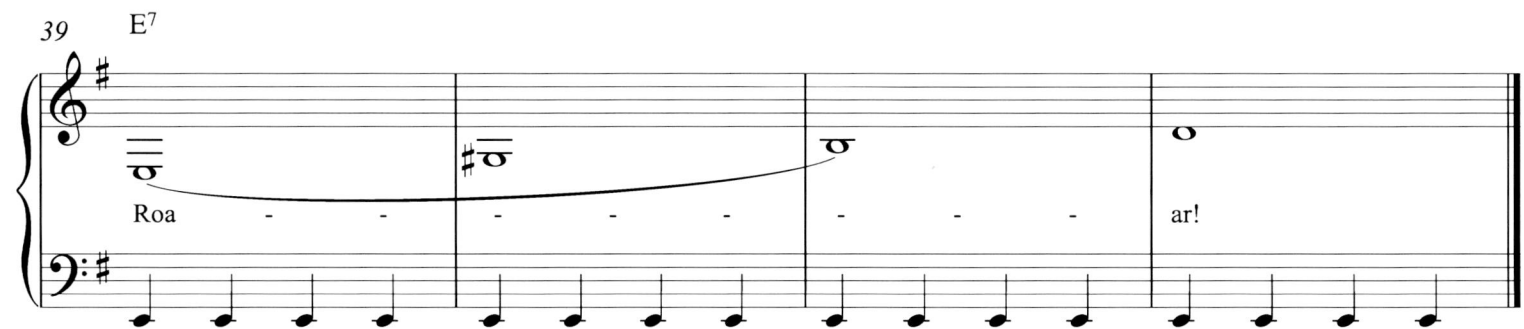

Doin' it
(Making the Garden Grow)

Words by Arthur Baysting
Music by Peter Dasent

♩ = 120
E E6 E E6 E E6 E E6
There's a
E E6 E E6 E E6
bum - ble bee, a ho - ney bee get - tin' the ho - ney for
E E6 A A6 A A6
you and me. Do - in' it, do - in' it. (Do - in' it, do - in' it.)
E E6 E E6 B7
Do - in' it, do - in' it. (Do - in' it, do - in' it.) Buzz - on' a - round

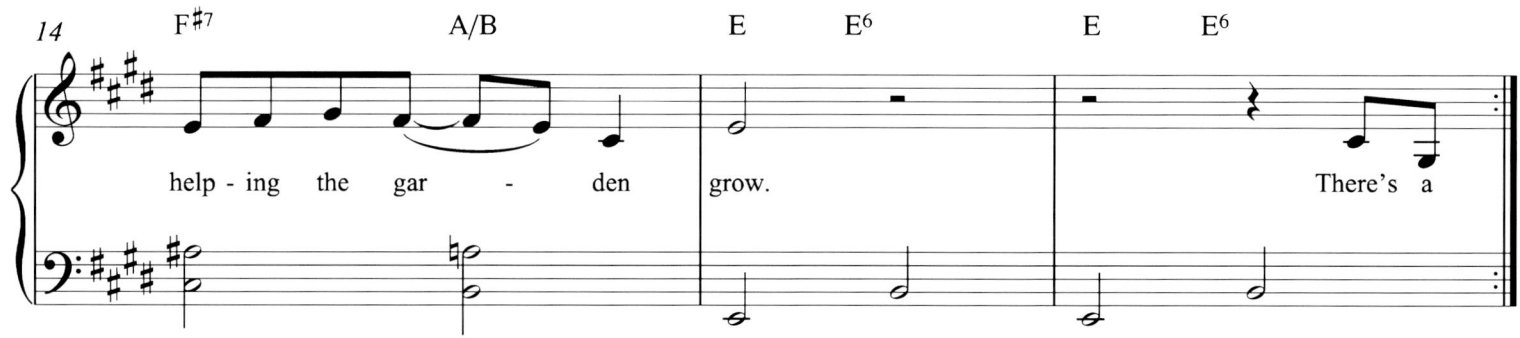

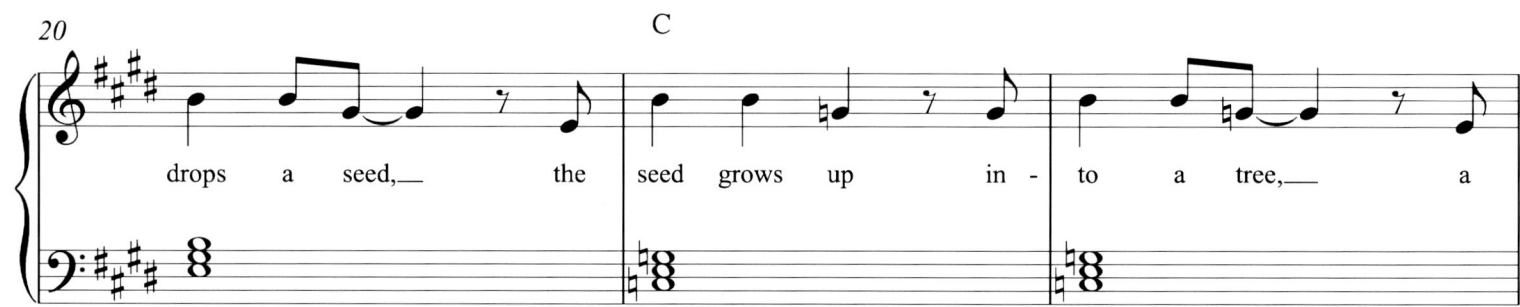

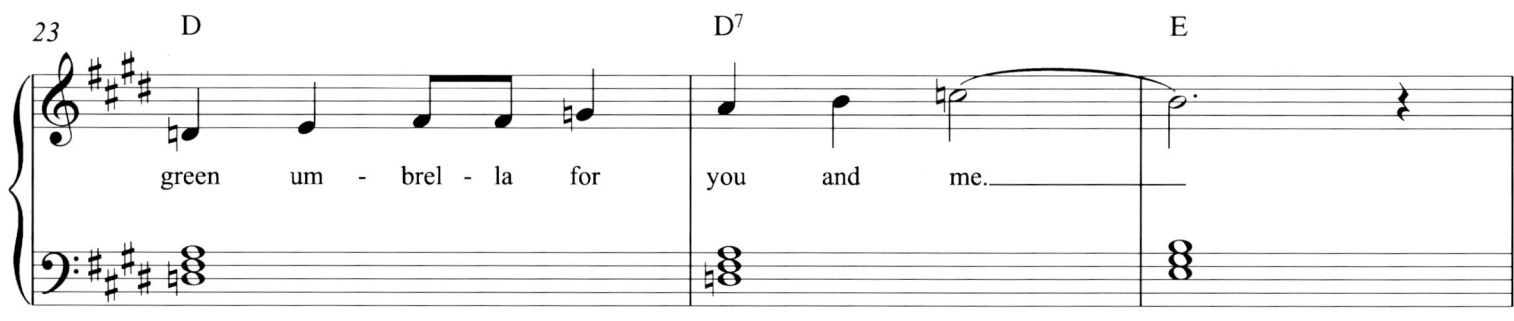

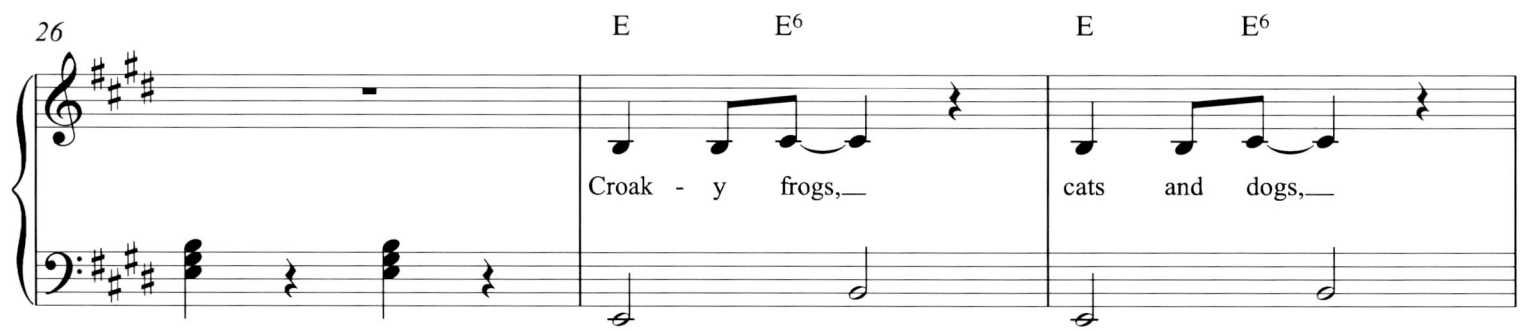

18

Great Big World

Words by Arthur Baysting
Music by Peter Dasent

There's a

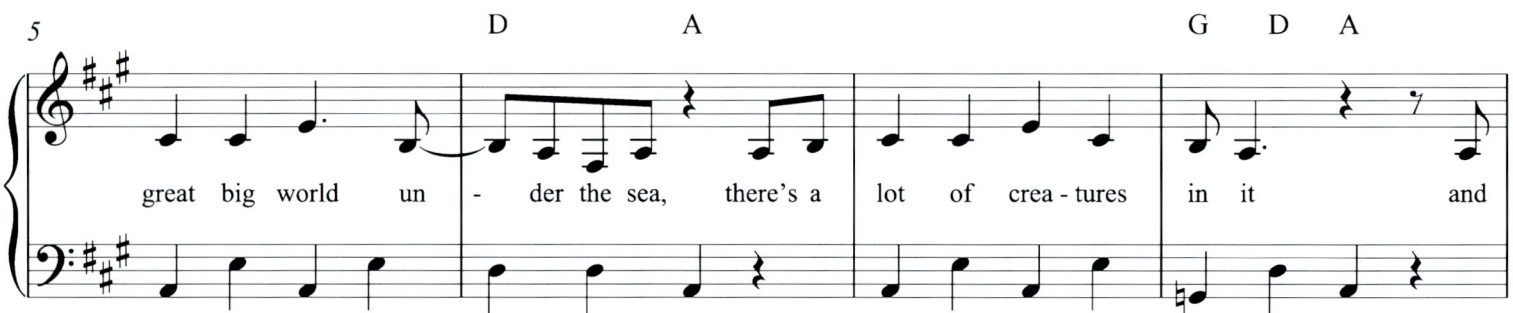

great big world un - der the sea, there's a lot of crea-tures in it and

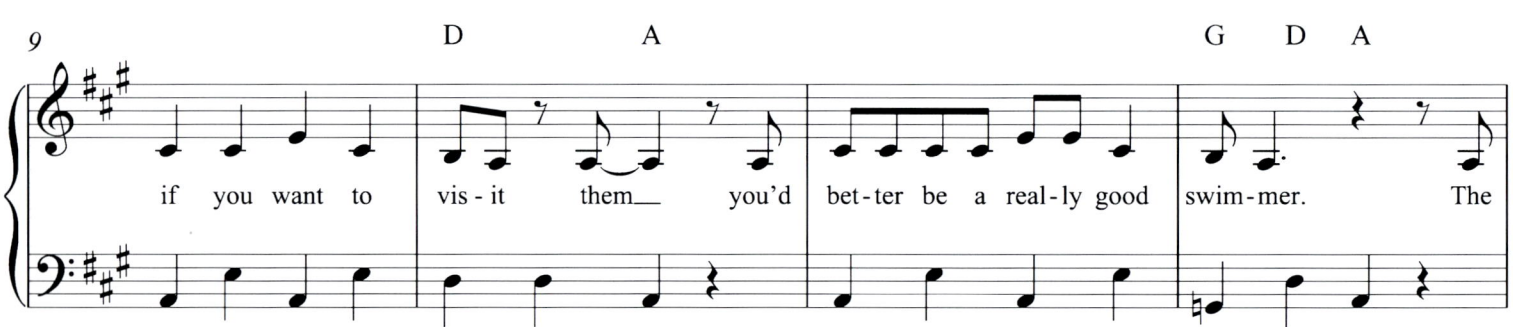

if you want to vis - it them___ you'd bet-ter be a real-ly good swim-mer. The

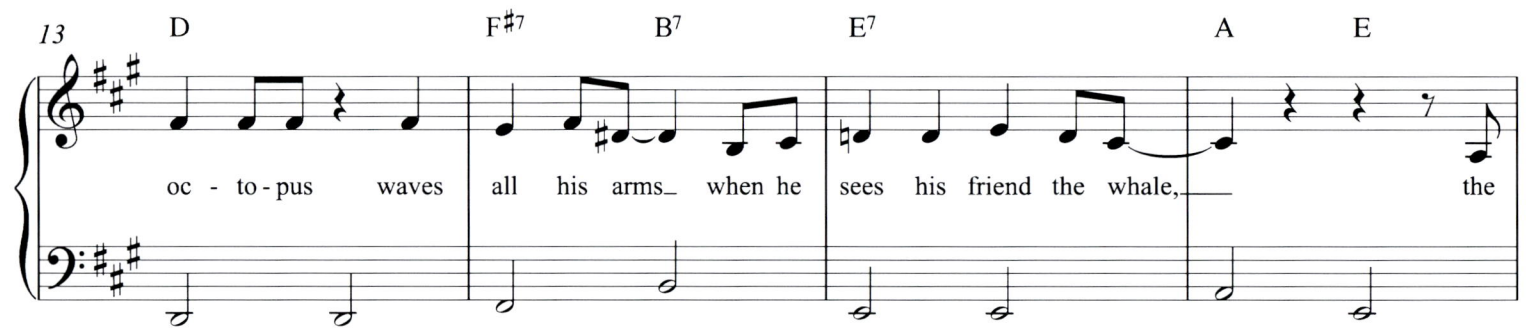

oc - to-pus waves all his arms___ when he sees his friend the whale,___ the

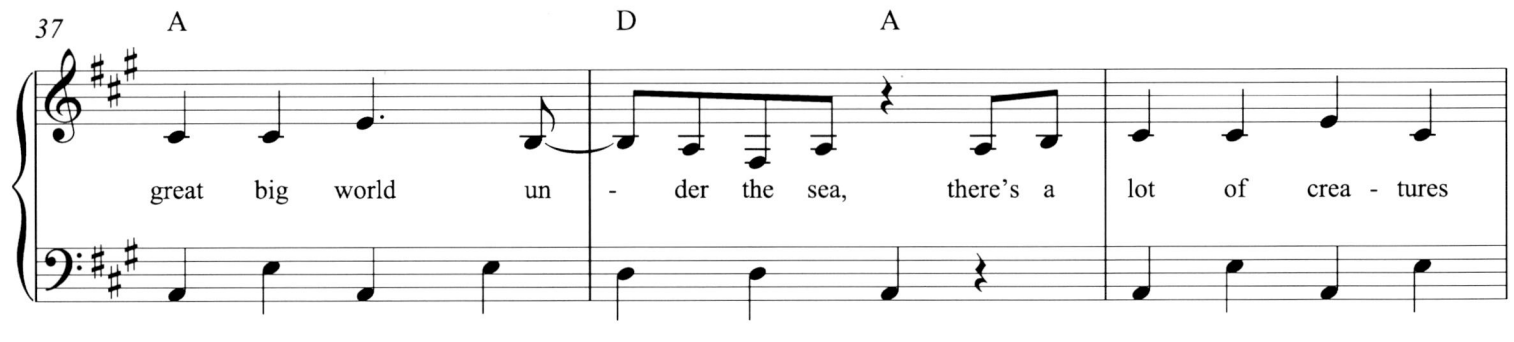

great big world un - der the sea, there's a lot of crea - tures

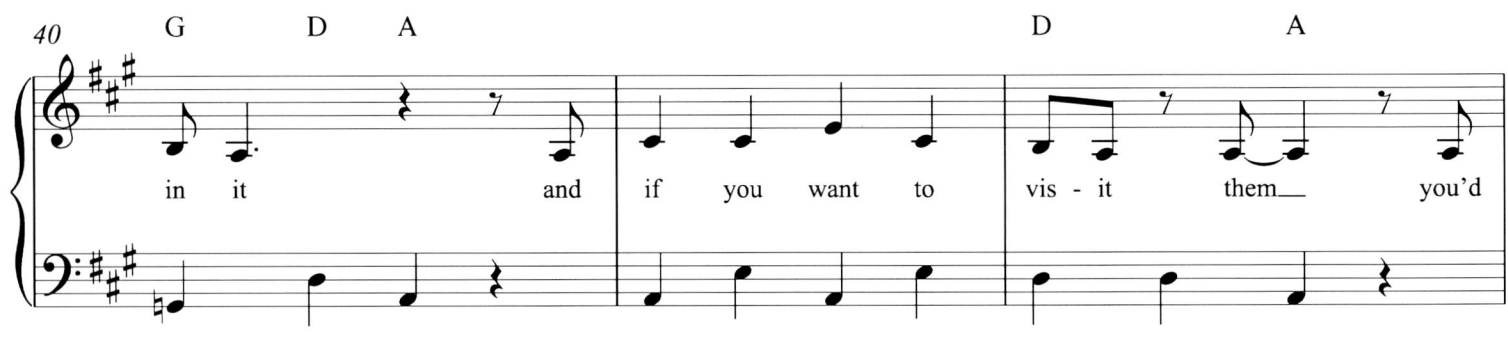

in it and if you want to vis - it them___ you'd

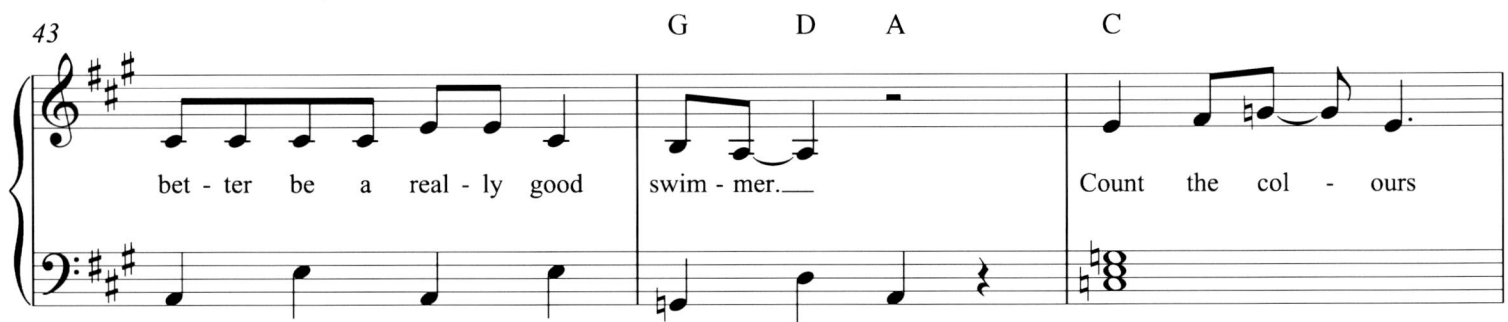

bet - ter be a real - ly good swim - mer.___ Count the col - ours

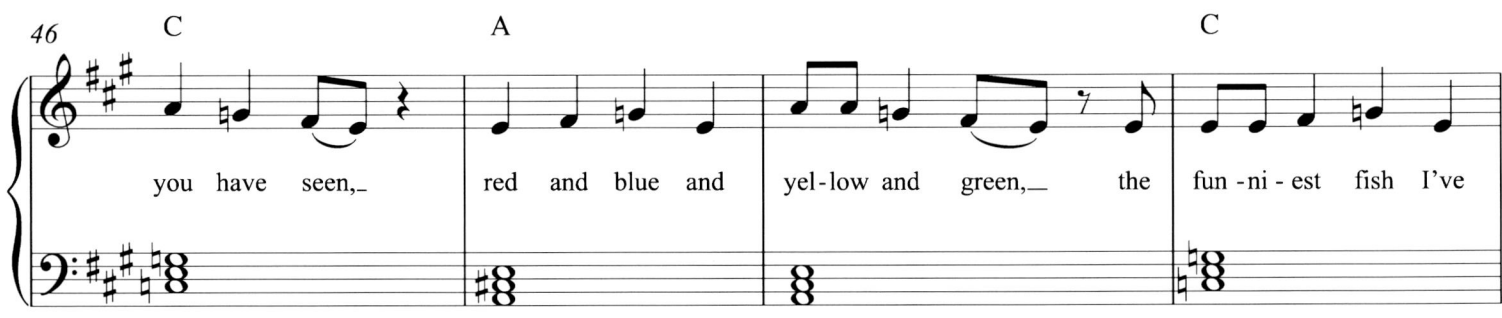

you have seen,_ red and blue and yel - low and green,_ the fun - ni - est fish I've

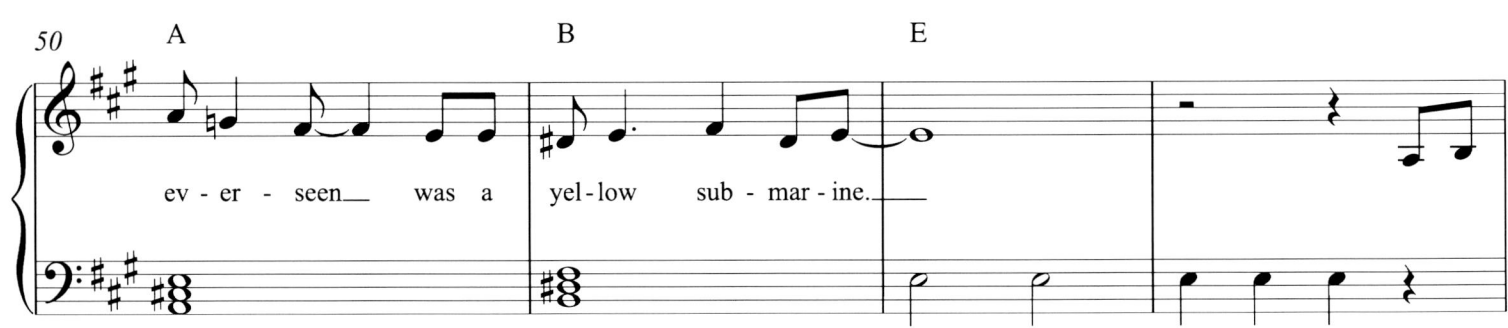

ev - er - seen___ was a yel - low sub - mar - ine.___

The Gum Tree Family

Words by Arthur Baysting
Music by Peter Dasent

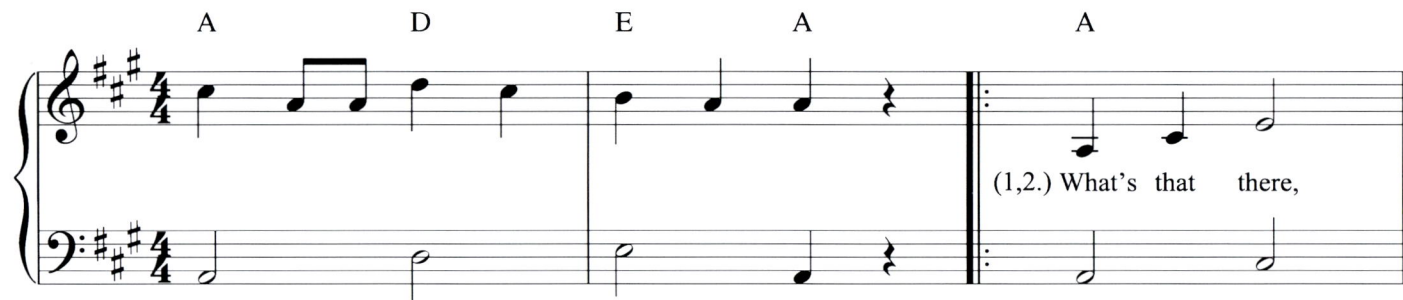

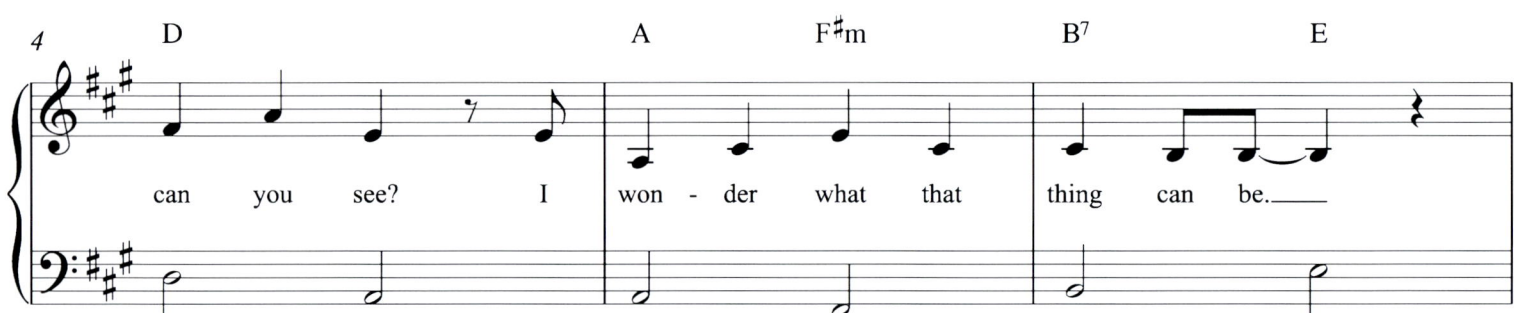

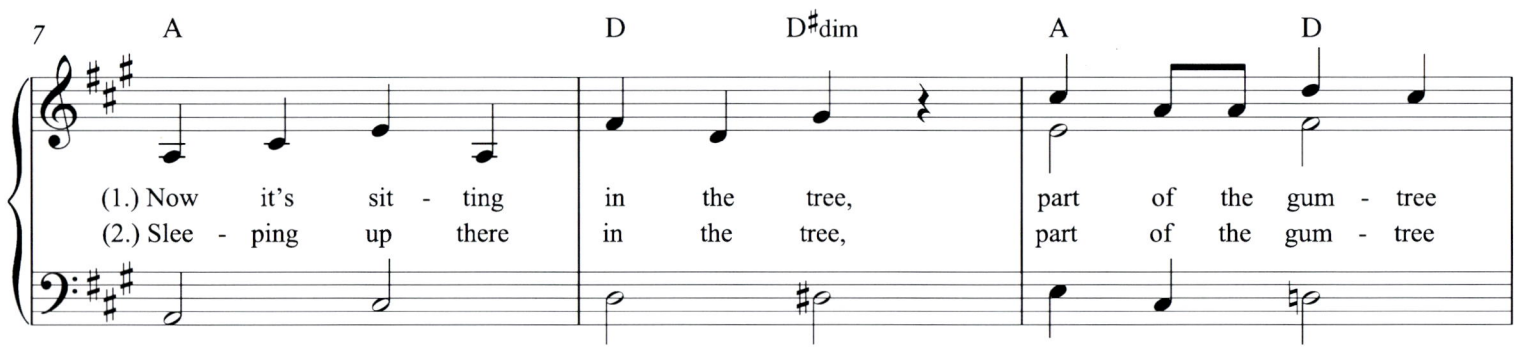

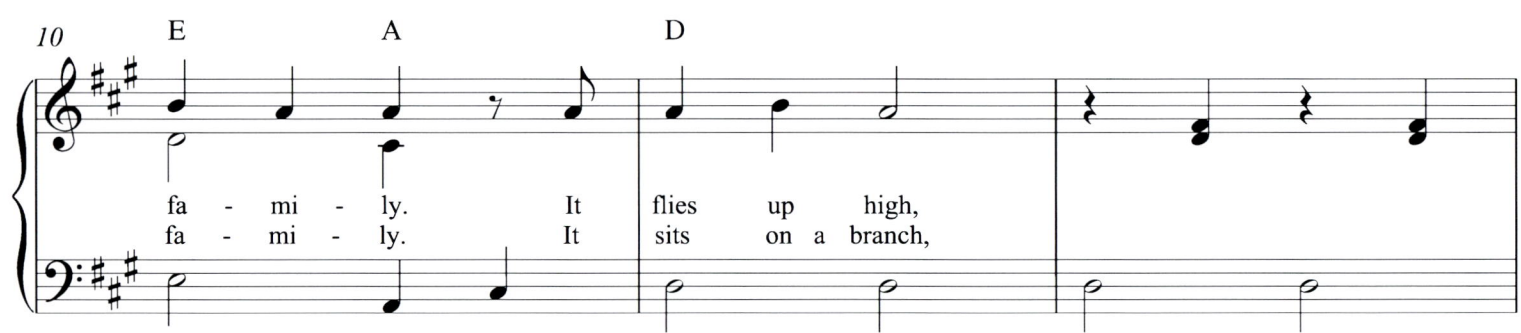

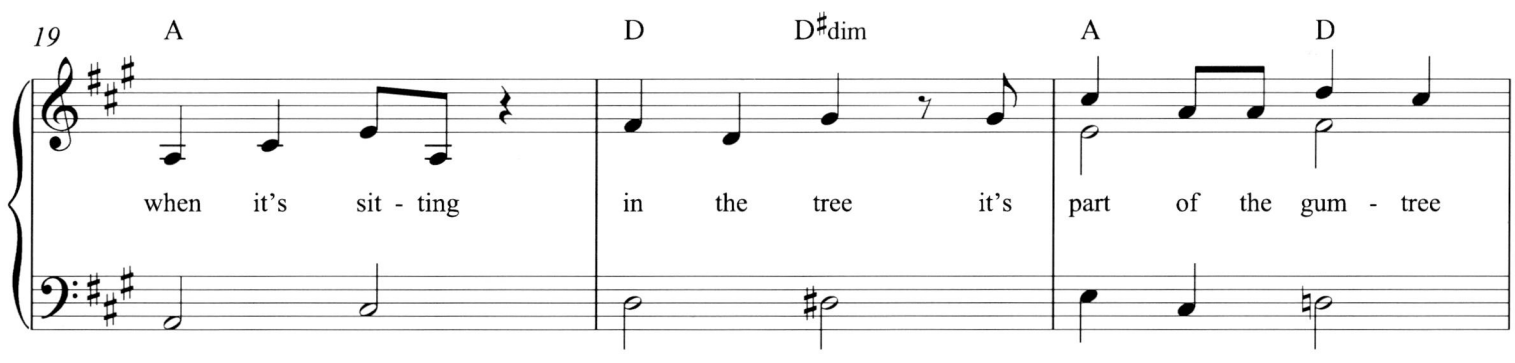

Hop Hippity Hop

Words by Garth Frost
Music by Peter Dasent

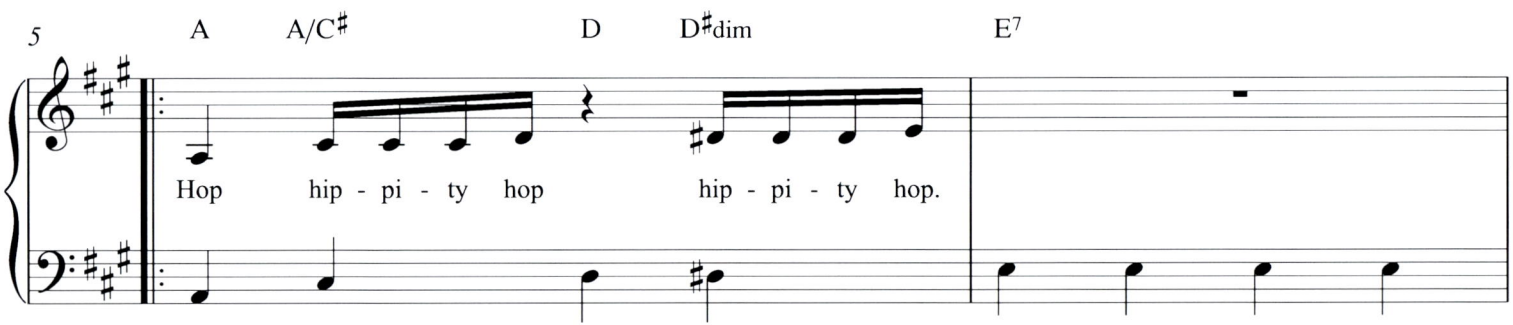

26

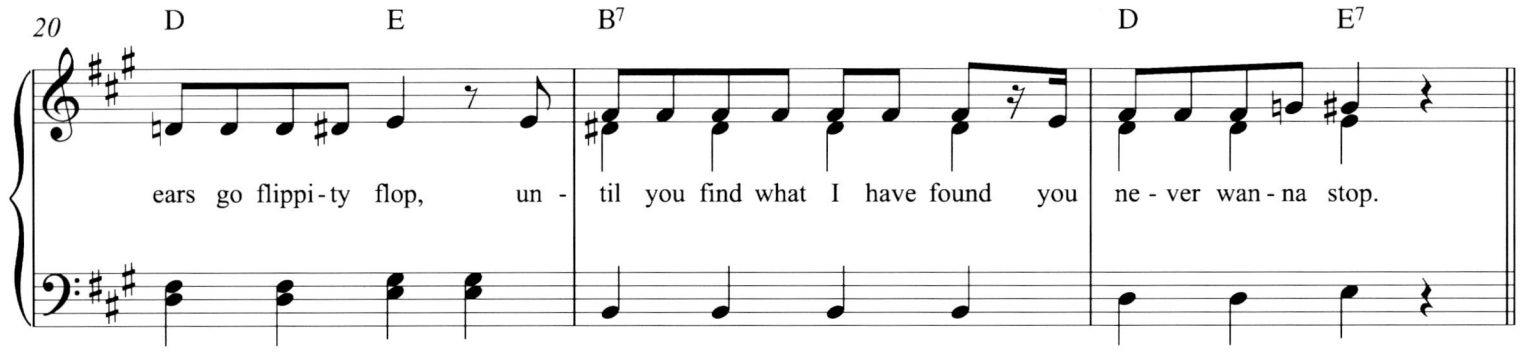

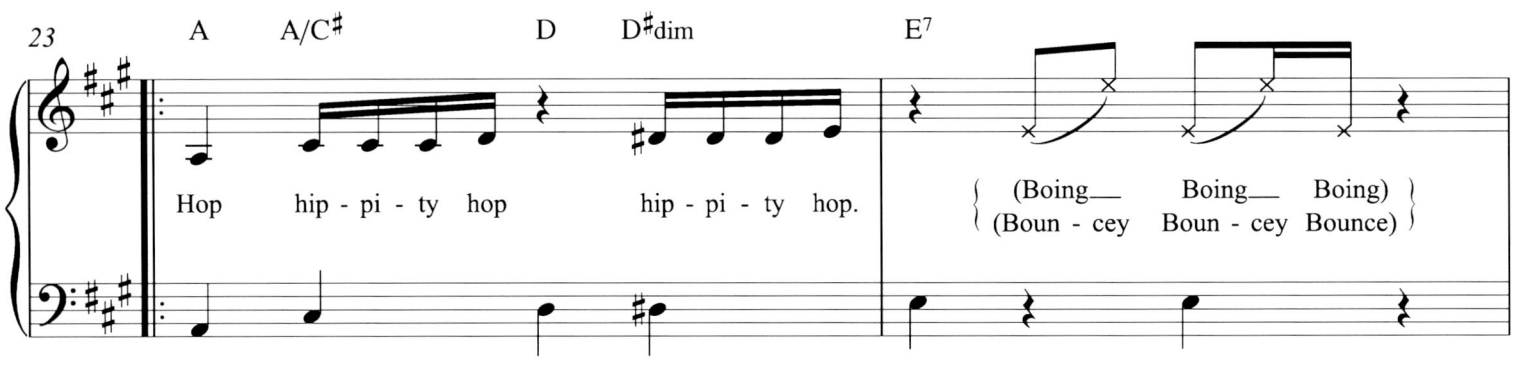

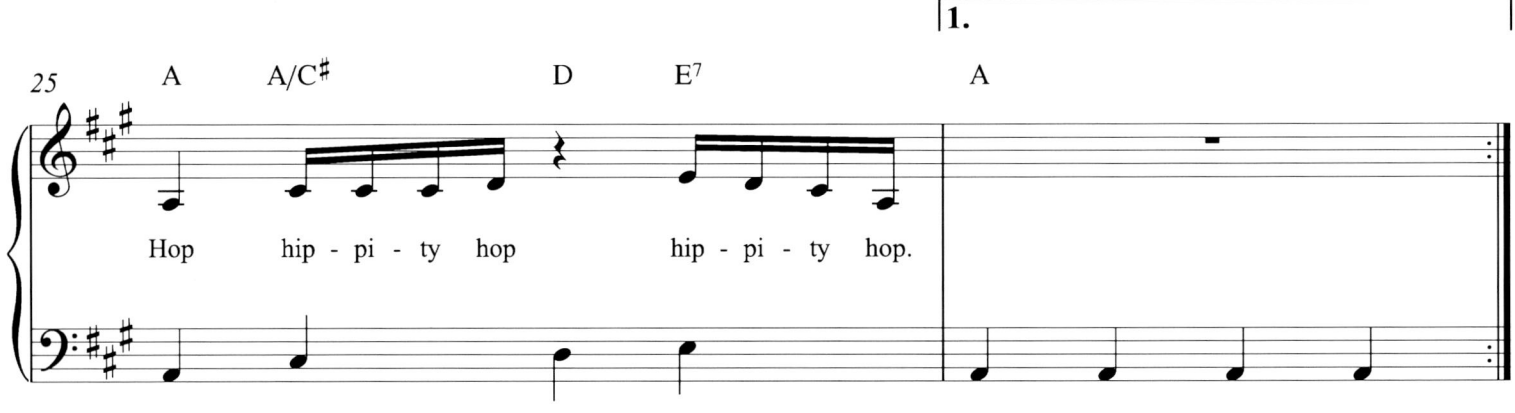

I Like to Sing

Words by Garth Frost
Music by Peter Dasent

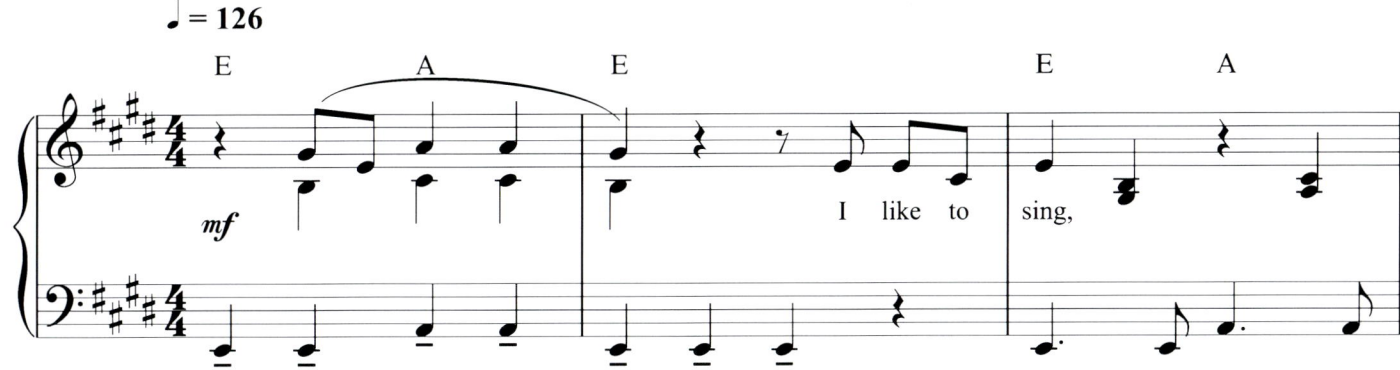

love it,   I love it,   I   real-ly real-ly do I like to dance.   I

like to do bal - let,   toes, on my toes, on my toes   and   swing all a-round.   Up and

down un - til I'm diz - zy but   then I'm real - ly hap - py with my

feet on the ground,   I like to   dance.   I like to

clap,
stomp,   Come - on!   Shake   the   floor!   I like to
shout hey!   Make   the   loudest   sound,   I like to
                                                    I like to

(chords 3° only)

It's My Birthday Today

Words by Arthur Baysting
Music by Peter Dasent

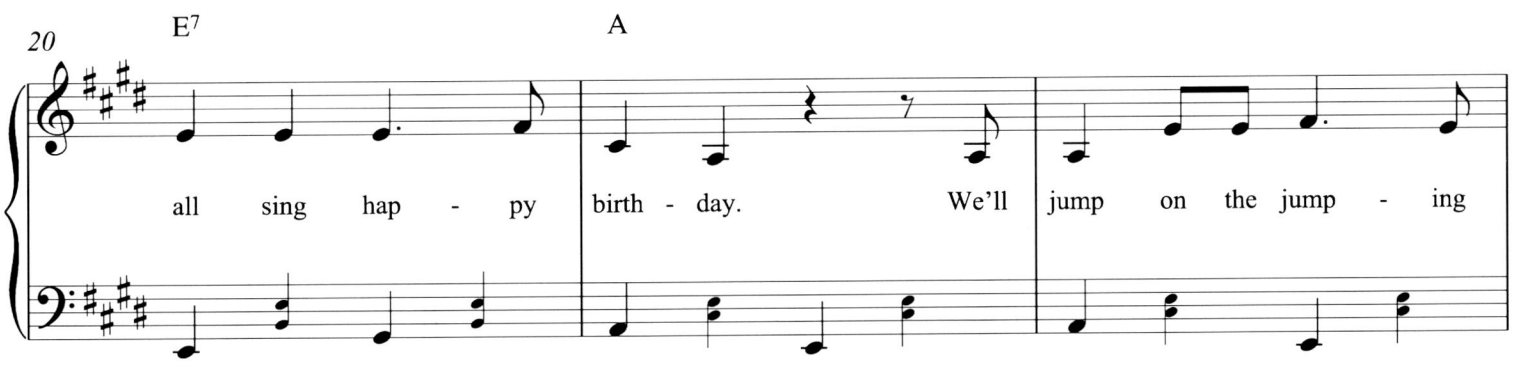

Little Day Out

Words by Arthur Baysting
Music by Peter Dasent

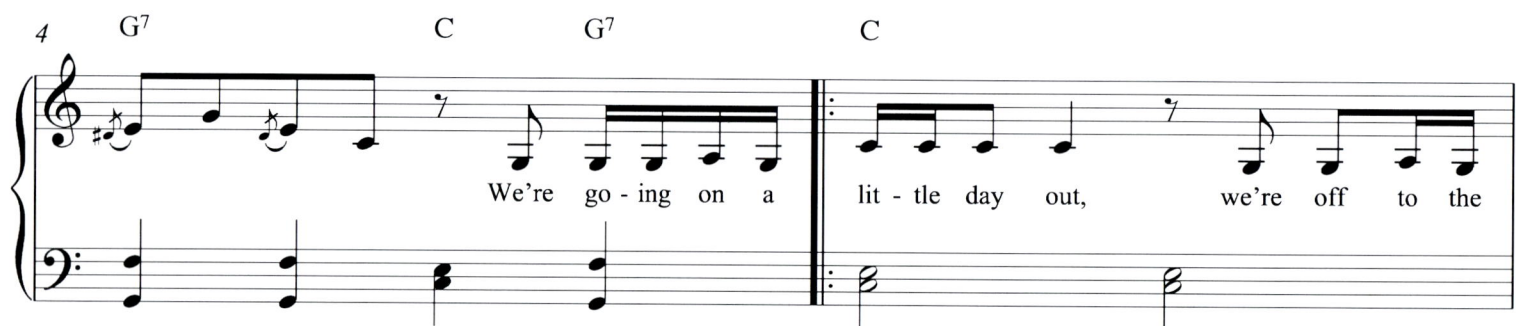

We're go - ing on a lit - tle day out, we're off to the

beach, we're gon - na swim in the sea, hear the sea - gulls screech.

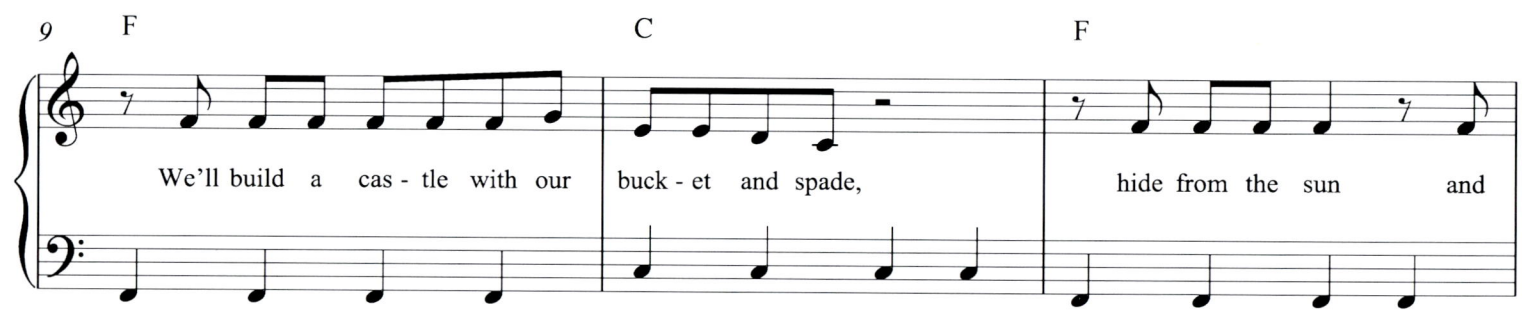

We'll build a cas - tle with our buck - et and spade, hide from the sun and

If I Had an Aeroplane

Words by Arthur Baysting
Music by Peter Dasent

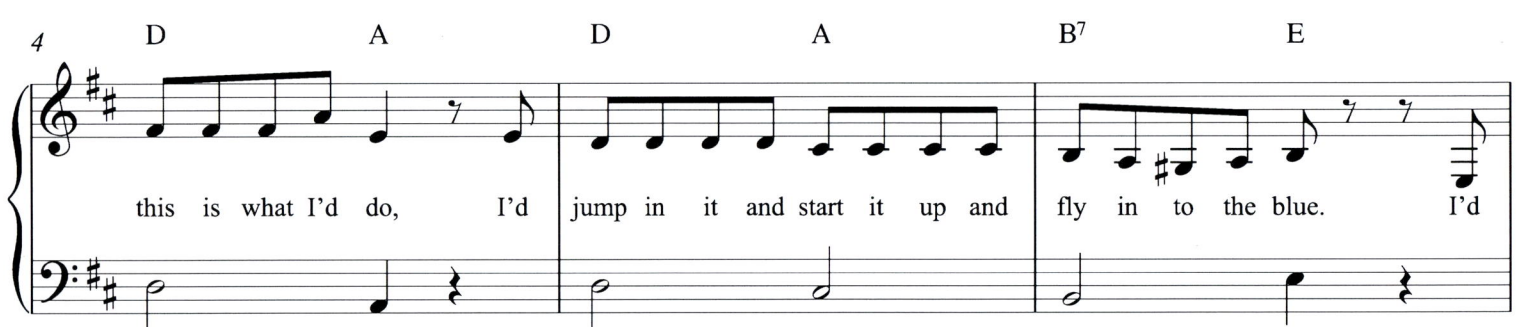

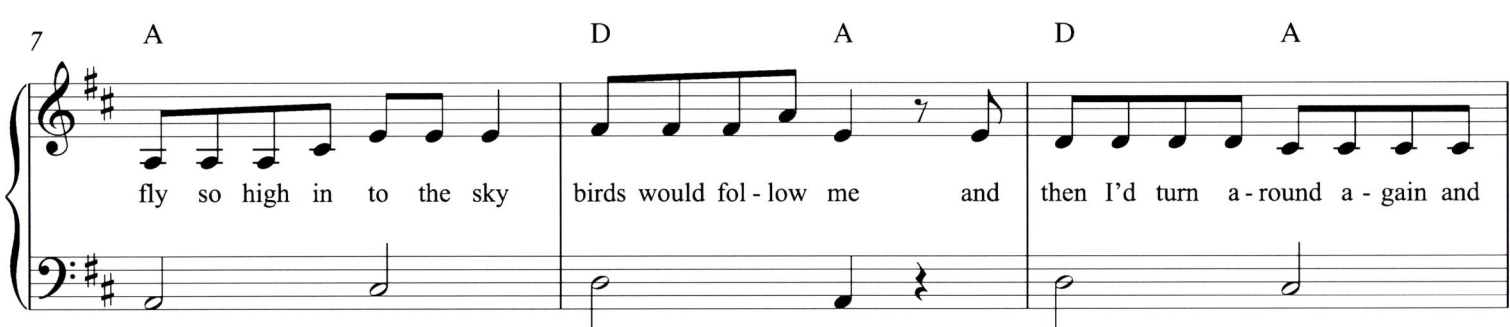

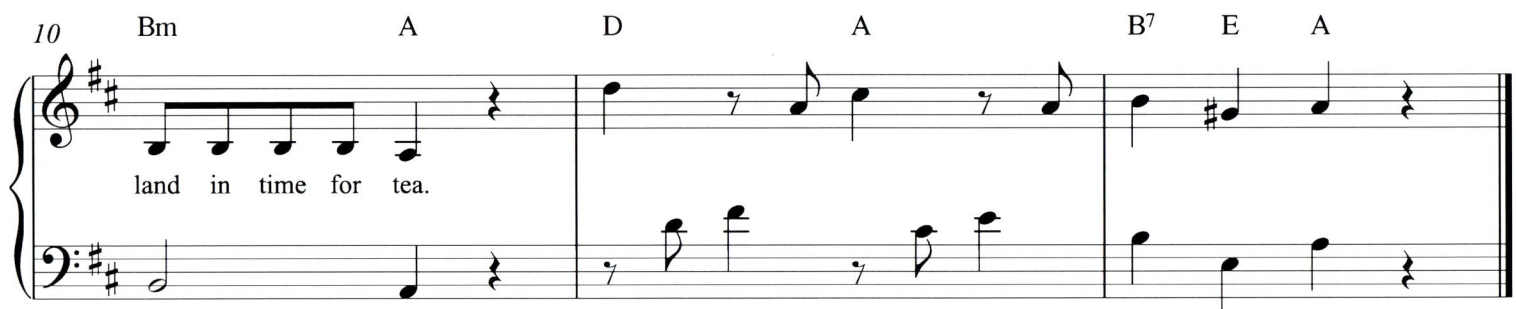

Mrs Knife & Mr Fork

Words by Arthur Baysting
Music by Peter Dasent

Gentle swing ♩ = 96

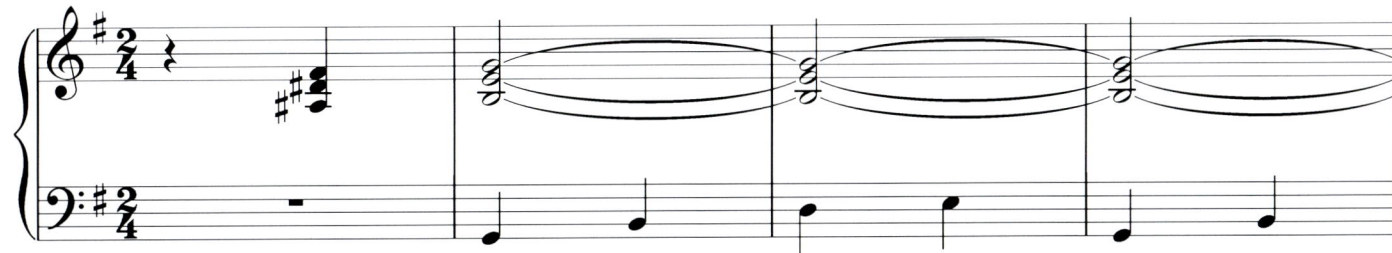

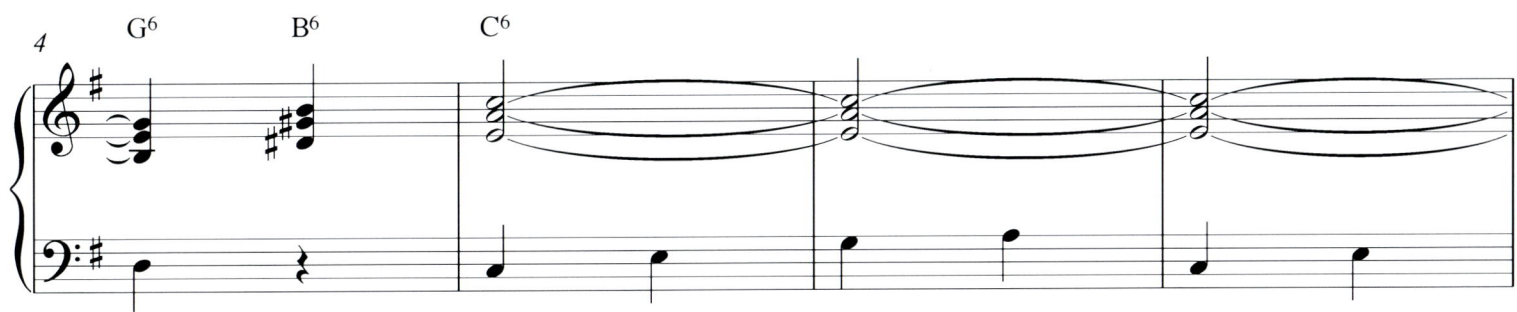

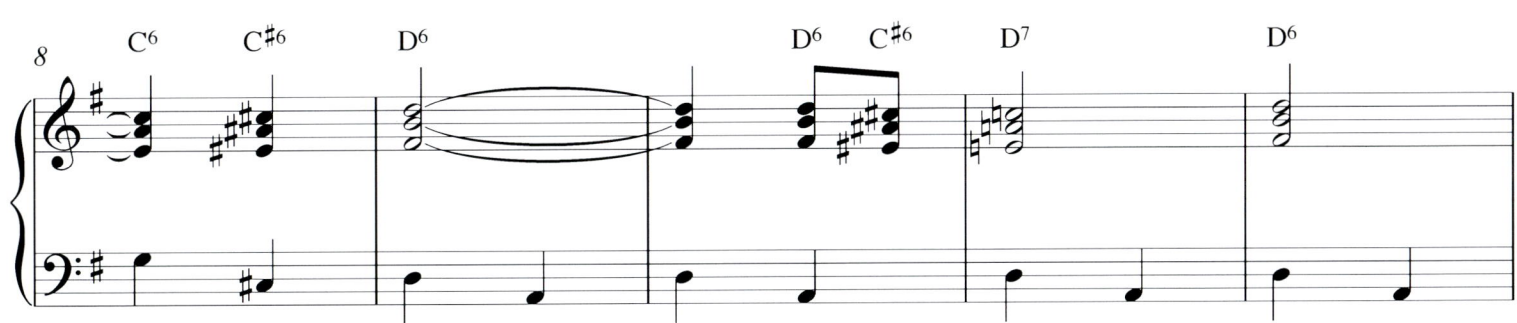

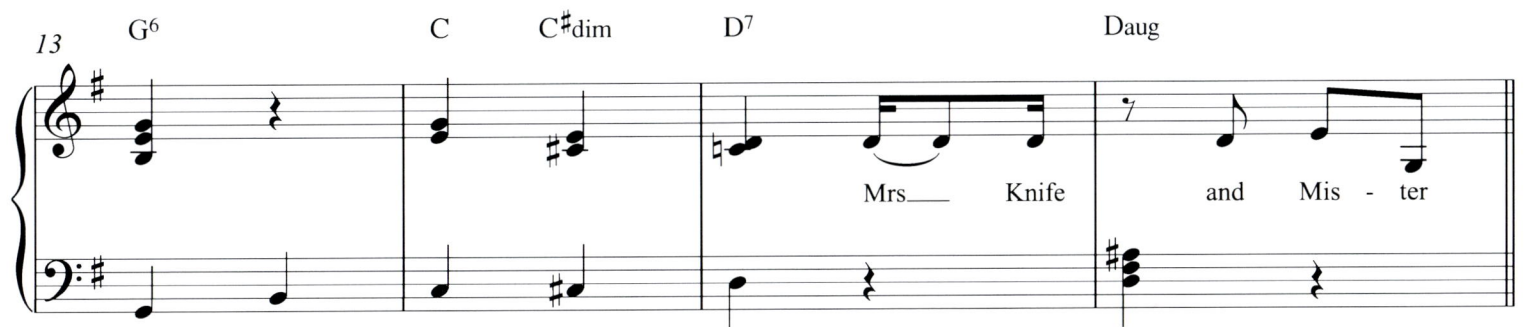

Mrs___ Knife   and   Mis - ter

dish - es a - way. Got - ta put those dish - es a - way.

Got - ta put those dish - es a - way. A - way, a - way,

— a - way, a - way, a - way.—

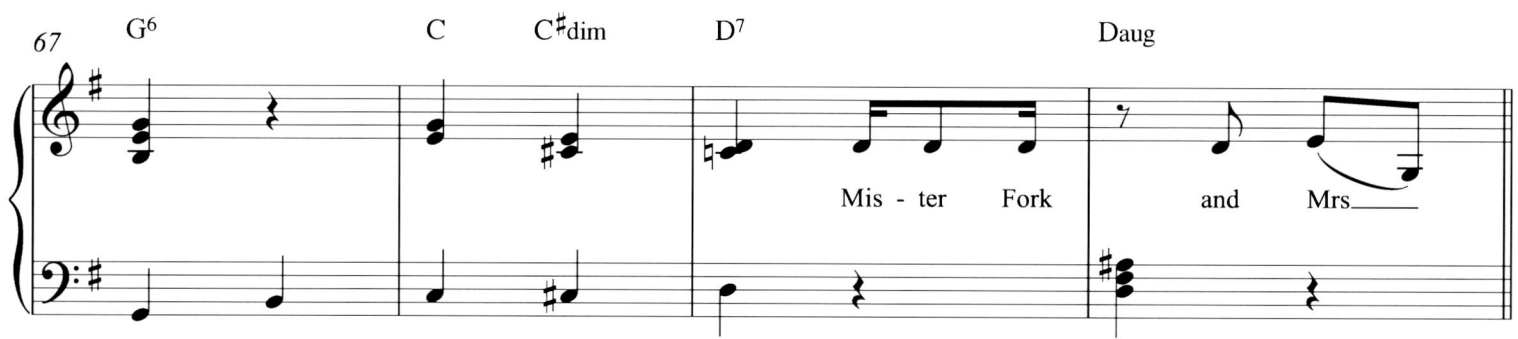

Mis - ter Fork and Mrs.—

Knife,
most,

just how hap - py can you
is when they've had their even - ing

Songs to Make you Smile

Words by Arthur Baysting
Music by Peter Dasent

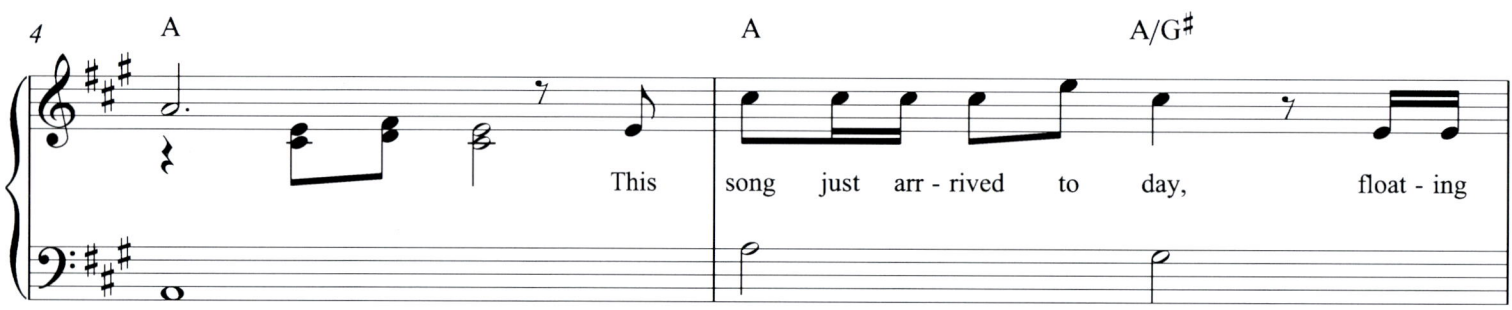

This song just arr-rived to day, float-ing

down from the mil-ky way, there's just one thing it wants to

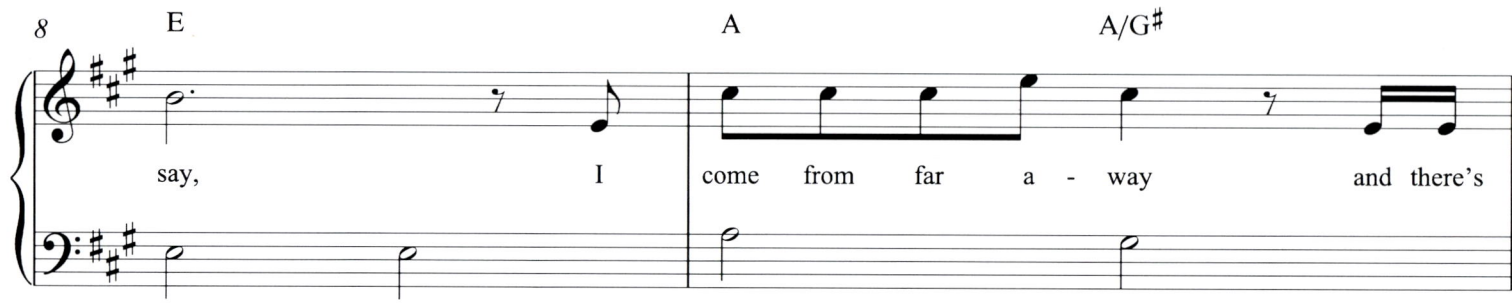

say, I come from far a-way and there's

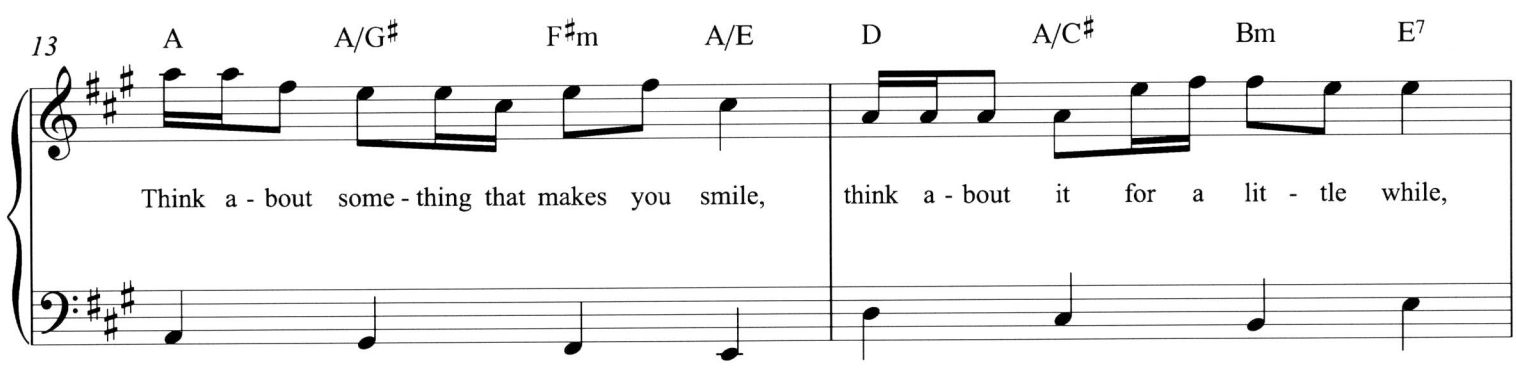

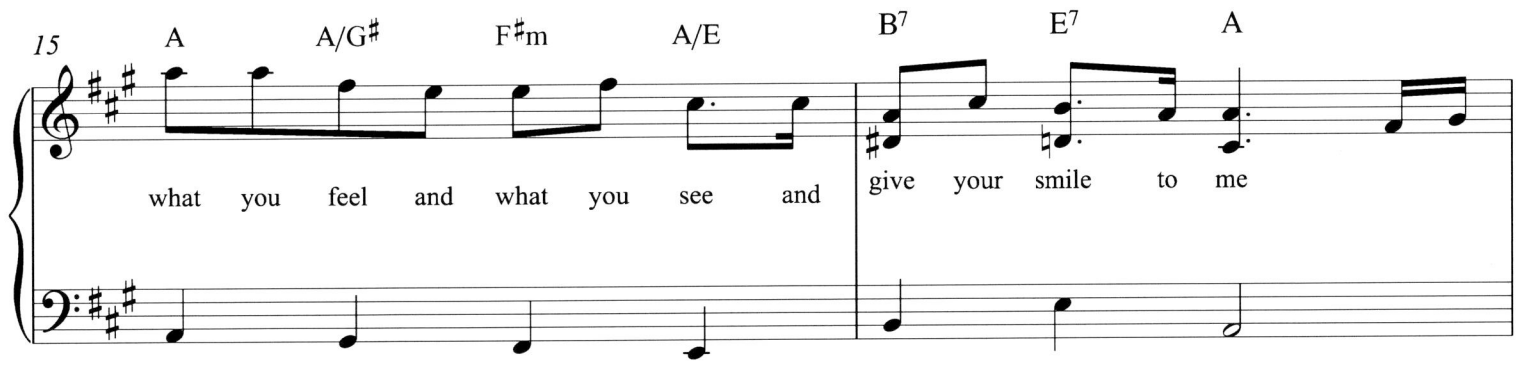

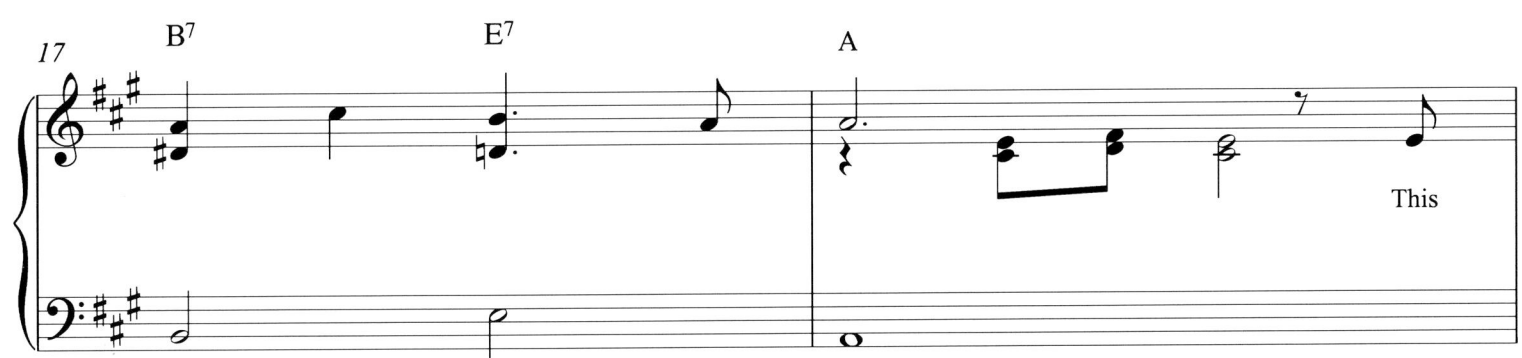

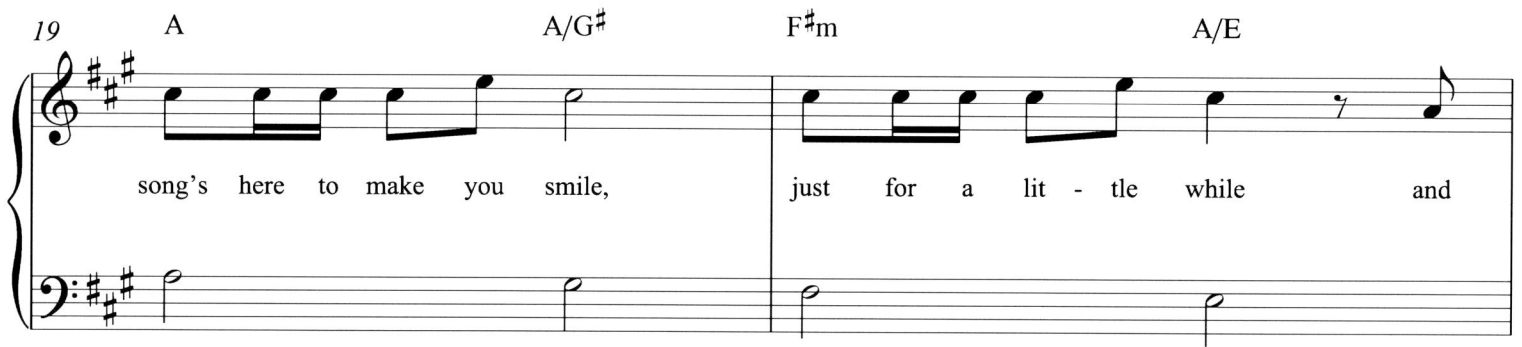

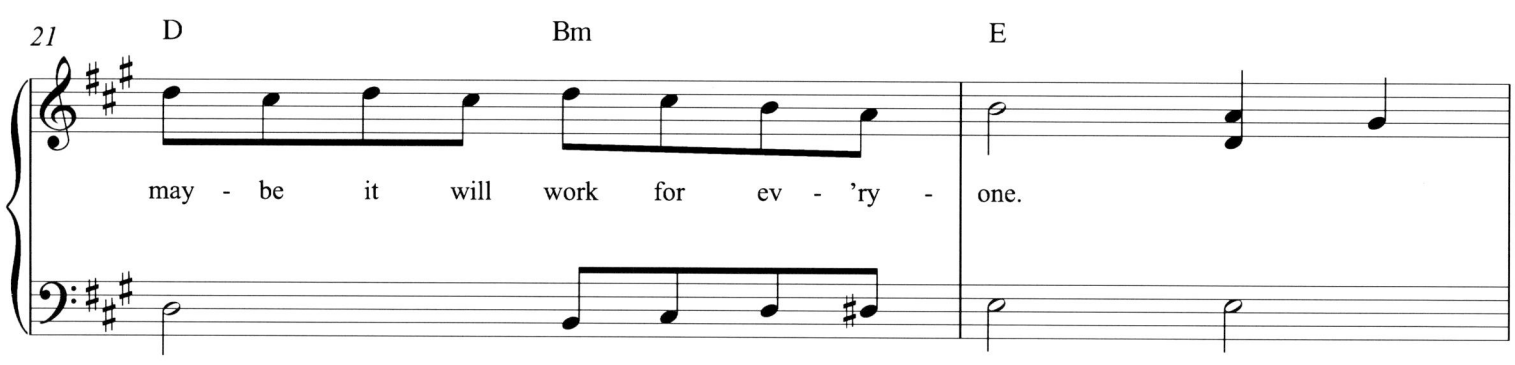

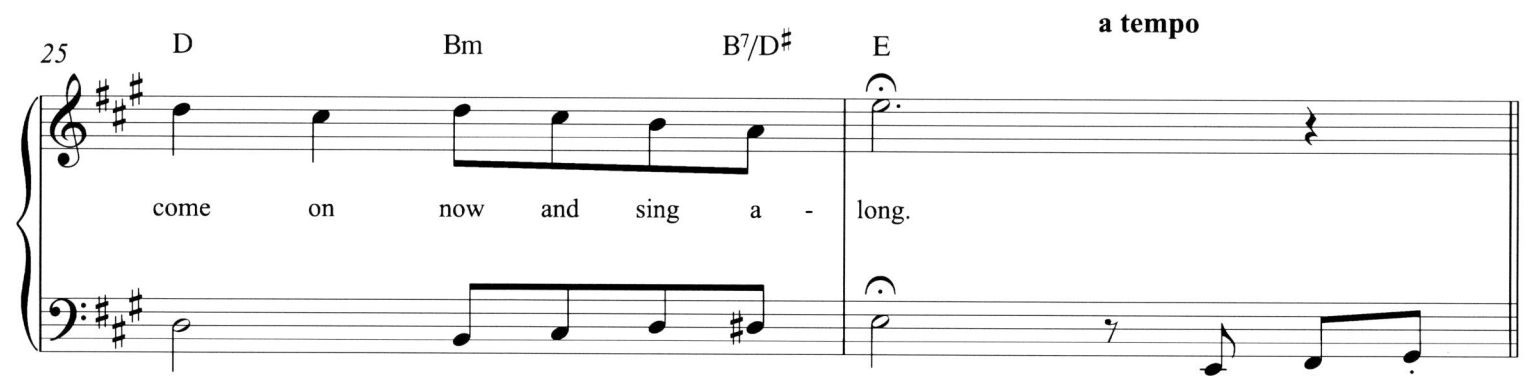

Watermelon

Words by Arthur Baysting
Music by Peter Dasent

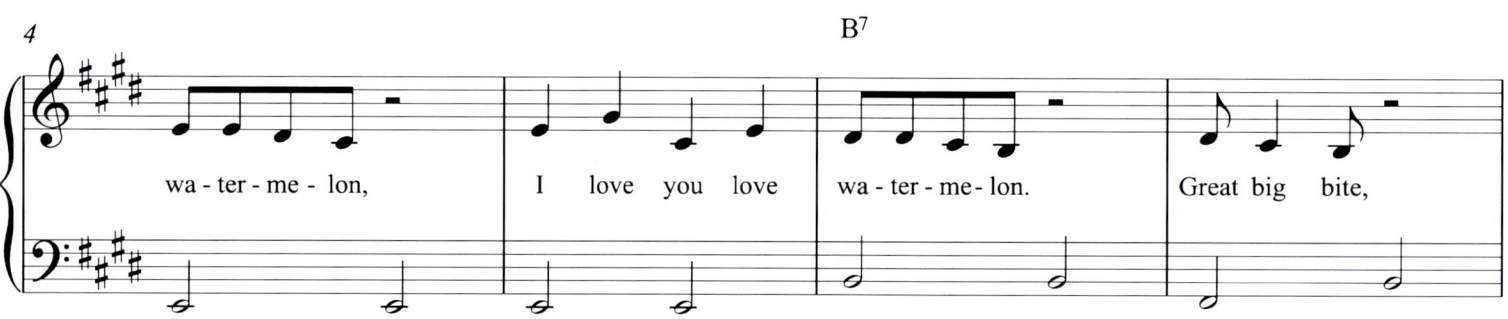

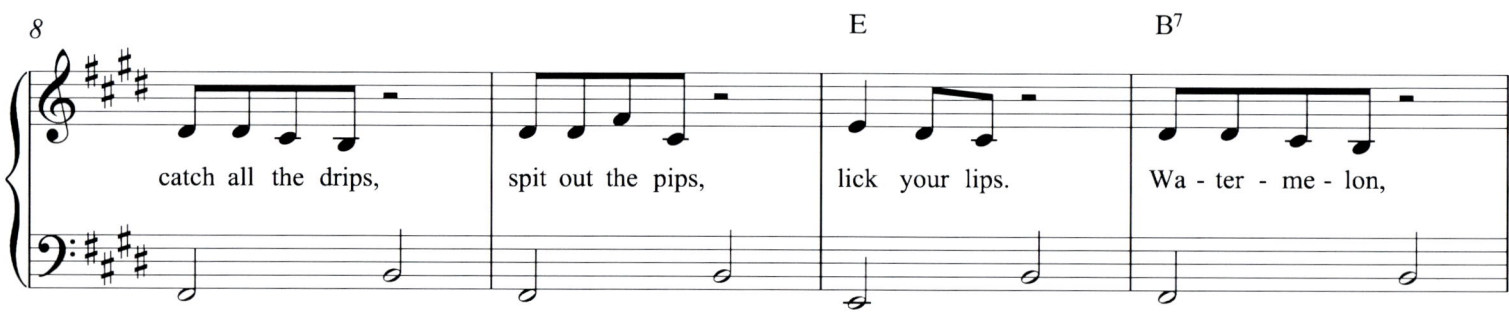

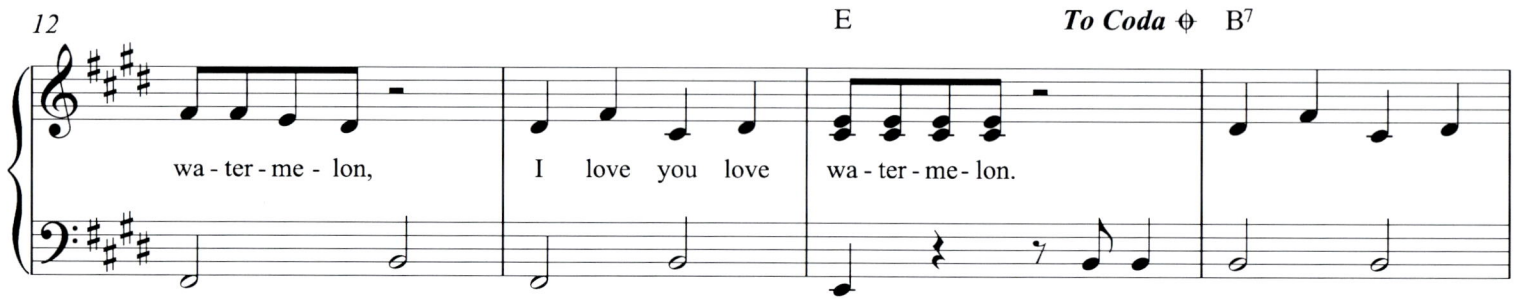

The Witches' Ball

Words by Arthur Baysting and Justine Clarke
Music by Peter Dasent

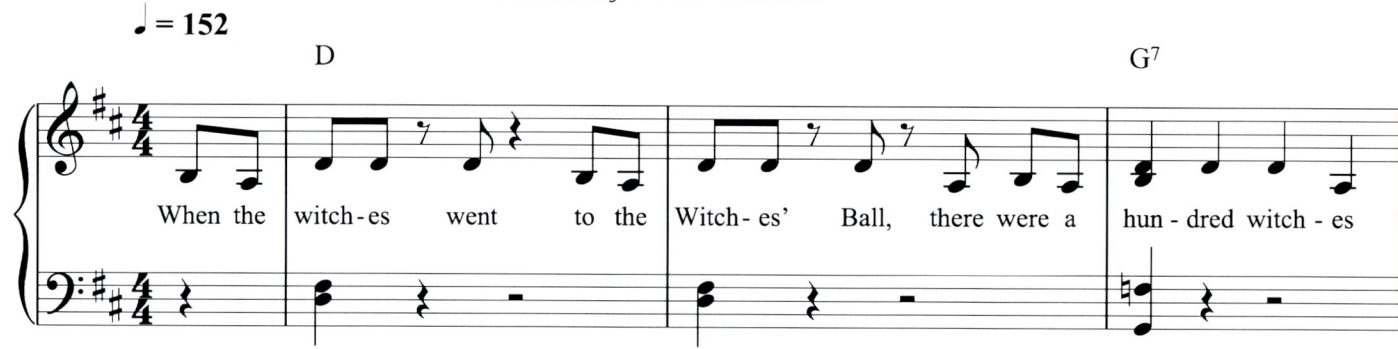

When the witch-es went to the Witch-es' Ball, there were a hun-dred witch-es

in the hall and all they did was scratch and scritch a - bout

which old witch was the witch - i - est witch. Witch - y Lou said to

Witch-y Sue, "You're just plain ug - ly" she said "Thanks you're ug - ly

too now let's go par - ty!" Well the place it just got

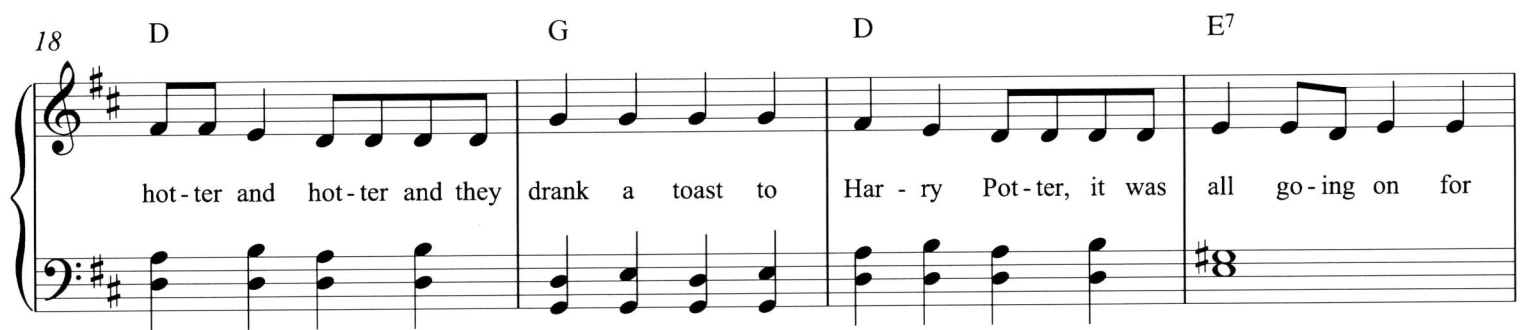

hot-ter and hot-ter and they drank a toast to Har - ry Pot-ter, it was all go-ing on for

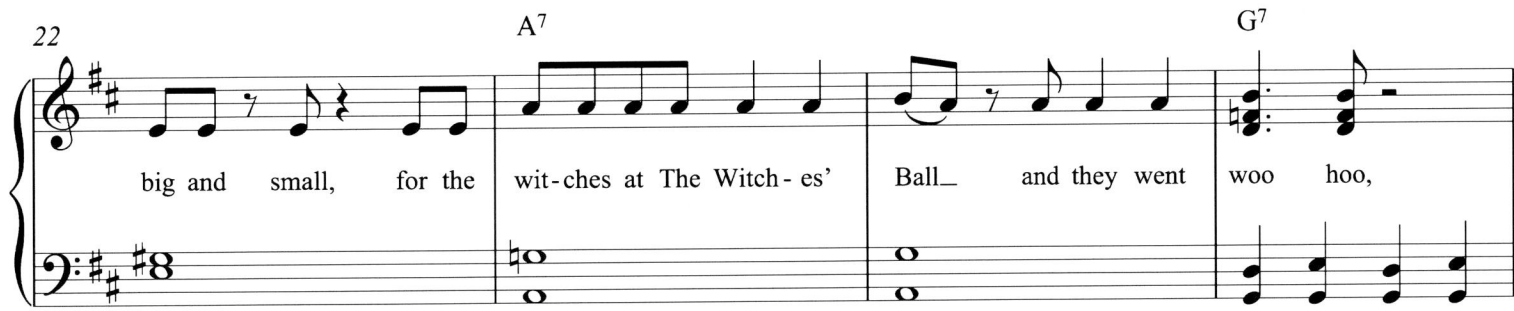

big and small, for the wit-ches at The Witch-es' Ball__ and they went woo hoo,

woo hoo, woo hoo, woo hoo, all the ghosts were fly - ing

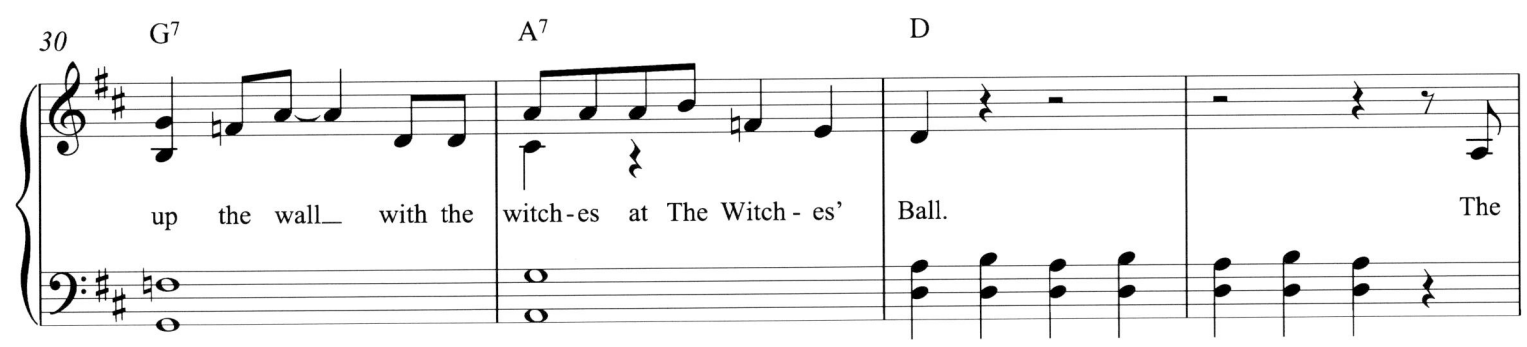

up the wall__ with the witch-es at The Witch-es' Ball. The

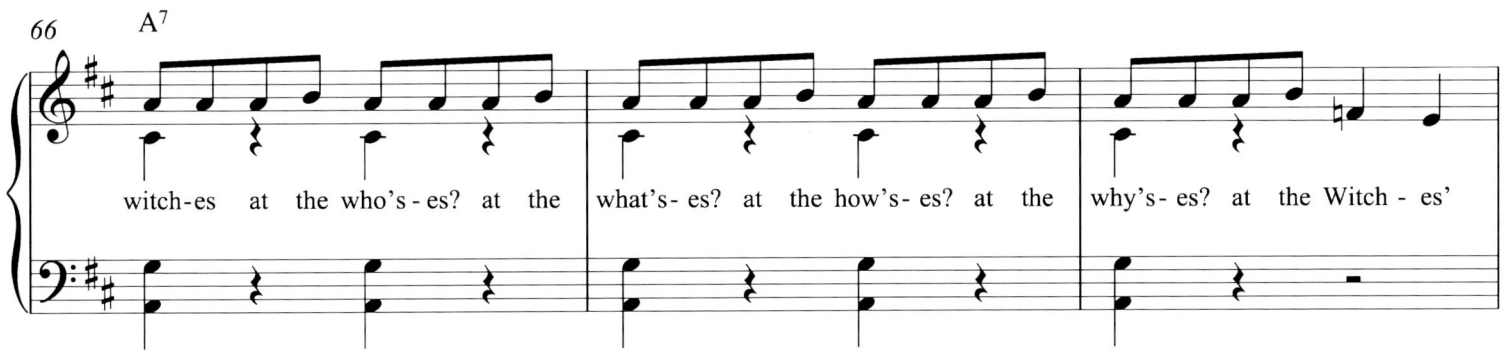

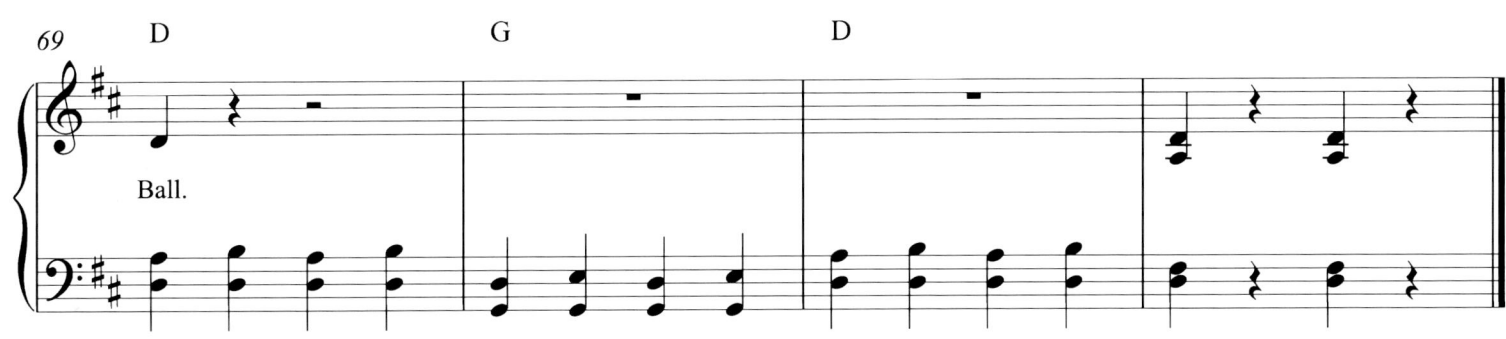

1 2 3 4 5 6 7 8 9

Activities

COLOUR IN

MATCH THE PAIRS

START

DOT TO DOT

SPOT THE MUSIC NOTES!

1. REMOVE PAGE FROM BOOK &
GLUE TO PIECE OF CARD FOR
EXTRA STURDINESS.
2. CUT OUT PIECES ON DOTTED LINE.
3. ATTACH STRING TO EACH PIECE.
4. TIE STRING TO PIECE OF DOWEL.
5. HANG.

MAKE A MOBILE